Were Chronicles

PACK COUNCIL

CRISSY SMITH

Pack Council
ISBN # 978-1-78686-366-9
©Copyright Crissy Smith 2018
Cover Art by Cherith Vaughan ©Copyright July 2018
Interior text design by Claire Siemaszkiewicz
Totally Bound Publishing

PACK COUNCIL

Dedication

A great big thank you goes out to my Sunday morning breakfast group who have listened to ideas and bounced around the plot with me. I enjoy our weekly meetings.

Prologue

Kurt rolled his neck, causing it to pop. His best friend, Clint, glanced over at him and grinned.

"Thanks for helping me finish remodeling," Kurt said. "Even if you did back out of buying the house with me."

"Hey!" Clint held up his hands. "It's not my fault. I told you I'd still pay for half."

Kurt waved Clint off. Yes, they had been supposed to move into together, but Clint had fallen in love with the cute coffee shop owner and had moved in with her instead. He had offered to still pay for the house, but the money wasn't what Kurt needed. He actually had more money than necessary. The Pack Council paid him well.

"Seriously," Clint said. "I didn't see the potential in this old place like you did, but damn, man, it looks amazing."

Kurt peered around. They were celebrating finishing the place with a barbecue in the back yard. From where he stood, he could see inside the kitchen where Clint's girlfriend was working on the sides for the meal. Kurt didn't know what he would have done without Clint or Sara. They'd been with him every step of the way. Sara had even used her green thumb to fix up the back yard.

The rose bushes were in full bloom. The other seasonal flowers and plants that she'd planted decorated the large area. He hoped they didn't all die on him. Sara had given him specific instructions on how to care for them.

"Hey, you still with me?" Clint smacked his shoulder.

"Just admiring my new place."

"You're a home owner. Who would have ever figured that?" Clint said.

"Who would have figured that you'd fall in love?" Kurt retorted.

Sara stepped out of the kitchen door at that moment. No surprise that Clint's gaze found her the moment she was outside. She stopped and kissed Clint before handing them both two fresh beers. She continued to where her dad, Sheriff Webb, was manning the huge barbecue grill.

"Yeah, things are really changing," Clint said.

They'd both accepted positions with the Alpha Council and now would be staying in one place for longer than a few months at a time. They were starting to put down roots once and for all. With Clint also settling down, he had even bigger ties to the community and wouldn't be going anywhere. Kurt would never leave Clint, so they'd be staying there.

Kurt found himself just a little bit jealous of his best friend, though. Clint had found a wonderful woman in Sara, and Kurt knew the two would be mating soon. Clint and Sara just fit together. Even mixing Clint's possessions in with Sara's already full house had been an experience in compromise and amusement. Kurt hadn't ever laughed so much as when he'd helped Clint move in.

It was a good day, so he buried any sad feelings deep inside and vowed just to enjoy the bright, warm sun and good company.

A couple of guards he and Clint worked with had dropped by to help. Ryan and his lover, Cecil, who was Sara's assistant at the coffee shop, had also stopped by and were now sharing a lounge chair in the middle of the yard.

Sara's dad had taken over preparing the steaks, burgers and hot dogs, refusing to let anyone else use Kurt's newest purchase. It had been one of the first things Kurt had bought for his house. Clint and Sara had gone with Kurt to pick it out, and Sara had been stunned by the size of the grill as Clint drooled over it on the showroom floor. Clint had just thrown an arm around her shoulder and explained that men needed meat, lots and lots of meat. Kurt already planned to purchase the same grill for Clint.

Kurt chuckled, remembering the day fondly. That was the day he'd known they'd made the right decision in accepting jobs with the Council. It had been past time to settle down. And they couldn't have picked a better place to do so. Both Kurt and Clint were now part of the community and the town residents had welcomed them with open arms.

"Any word from Colt?" Clint asked quietly beside him, pulling him from his thoughts.

Kurt shook his head. Over a month ago, a chapter of the Church for Humanity had moved into the area. The Church's preacher, Dan Carter, had never made an appearance, but Carter's second-in-command, Perry

Costa, had been nothing but trouble. Protesters had lined the small town's streets, holding signs and cursing shifters. Perry had also been behind Clint's kidnapping.

Perry had wanted to be turned into a shifter and had taken Clint to try to force Clint to bite him. Clint had bitten Perry — and the two men helping him — but since a shifter bite couldn't turn a human into a shifter, obviously Perry hadn't gotten what he'd wanted. Perry and the two men who'd helped him had been arrested along with the deputy who'd been involved. The Church was still around, but luckily the protests had stopped and there hadn't been any more attacks.

It might have only been a few months since the world had become publicly aware of shifters, but Kurt hoped the publicity died down soon. Too many Packs had had to deal with threats to their families.

The shifters had won the battle with Perry Costa, but Kurt worried about the next time. The war was far from being over. They'd managed to fight the Church and Perry because they had an inside man. Colt, a Beta from one of the Colorado Packs, had gone undercover to keep an eye on the Church.

"Tony said Colt sent him a couple messages but hasn't been able to get much out of him. Just that Colt's on to something and will get back to him."

"Damn, I hope he's okay."

Kurt did too. Colt was a good man who was placing himself in danger to make sure all the other shifters remained safe.

"You think Tony and Colt will be okay after this? It's quite a task Colt is taking on," Clint said.

Kurt grinned. "I'd bet a month's pay that there's a strong enough relationship there. I think they'll be okay."

Clint nodded. "I don't know how Tony can stand for him to be in constant danger." Clint looked toward Sara. "I would go insane."

"Yeah." Kurt could only agree. If Kurt was lucky enough to find a mate, he didn't think he would be able to let her out of his sight. He'd come close to mating once. He'd been young and she'd been even younger. He'd somehow known he wasn't ready and had joined the military instead, breaking off the relationship.

Now that he'd retired, he thought back on that time in his life—how different it would have been if he had stayed, mated Becca and started a family.

Becca had recently found her true mate. And she was so in love with Mike Jackson that Kurt knew he had made the right decision. But sometimes he wished things had ended differently—that he had someone waiting at home for him.

He gazed out over the yard. These people were part of his family now. Sara, her dad, Ryan and Cecil, and the guards, Sam and Colin—they were the ones he could depend on and vowed to protect. To love in his own way.

Sara was laughing at something her dad had said. Clint's eyes were locked on her. It seemed that Clint always knew where Sara was. Kurt wanted that kind of love. Sara saw them looking at her and blew a kiss to Clint. Kurt's heart ached. He didn't want his buddy's girl, just what Clint had with her, what Becca had with Mike. He hoped it wasn't too late for him.

He must have sighed or something, because Clint elbowed him. "Those are some heavy thoughts," he commented.

Kurt took a long pull of his beer and nodded but didn't share.

"Savannah!" Sara's cry drew both men's attention. She rushed across the yard and threw her arms around the shoulders of the newcomer, hugging her tight.

Once she had pulled away, Kurt got his first look at the new guest. A beautiful blonde stood with Sara, laughing at something Sara was saying. Sara pointed back toward him and Clint and the woman looked over.

Kurt's breath caught when his gaze locked on hers. She was taller than Sara. She had pale, flawless skin, bright, large blue eyes and a wide, welcoming smile. His cock immediately came to attention.

Damn, she's gorgeous! "Who's that?" he murmured to Clint.

Clint chuckled. "That, my friend, is the newest deputy. She is also one of Sara's best friends. She just moved back to town, as a matter of fact."

Kurt felt the need to pour the cold beer over his head to cool down when the two women started over. His cock was hard, trapped behind the zipper of his jeans, and his canines ached to release.

Oh, this is very interesting.

Clint gripped his shoulder. "If you can stop drooling long enough for me to introduce you..."

Kurt cleared his throat. *Yeah, that sounds like a damn good idea.*

Savannah was doing her best to pay attention to what her friend was saying but just couldn't pull her gaze away from the attractive dark-haired man in front of her.

"Kurt Moore," he greeted and held out his hand.

She slipped her palm into his and felt a jolt of something throughout her body. He gave her hand a squeeze before he released her, and she had to curl her fingers to keep herself from reaching back for him. He had a sparkle of amusement in his gaze, but she didn't mind. He seemed to be checking her out as much as she was him. She was a bright girl and knew what she wanted with this man. Savannah always got what she wanted.

The man next to Kurt said something and Savannah had to shake herself out of her appreciation and respond. "I'm sorry?"

Clint—she remembered Sara's boyfriend's name— grinned. "So, you made it back to town okay?"

"Yes, it's really good to be home."

"How do you know Sara?" Kurt questioned in that deep voice.

Mmm, she liked the sound of him talking. Goosebumps broke out on her arms. She was pretty sure his lifted eyebrow was an indication that he knew what she was thinking.

"Oh!" Savannah waved a hand. "I met Sara when we both wanted to play with the same building blocks in kindergarten. All the other girls wanted to play with the dolls. But not us." She grinned at Sara. "We fought about who got the best Legos."

Sara and the two men laughed along with her.

"And Savannah always ended up with them," Sara complained good-naturedly.

"That's because I cheated," Savannah told her with a wink.

Sara rolled her eyes while Clint wrapped his arm around her shoulder. "I'll buy you the best Legos out there. As many as you want," he promised. Sara beamed up at him and the love between Sara and Clint was so obvious that she felt like a voyeur.

"Why don't we let these love birds get all mushy together?" Kurt joked. "Can I get you a drink?"

"Yes, please." She wrapped her hand around Kurt's arm and let him lead her toward the patio door.

It had been almost five years since she'd been back in Lovington. On her last visit, Sara had just returned to town from school and was still staying with her dad. Savannah was horrible at keeping in touch. She needed to get better at that. Now that she was home, she hoped she could reconnect with Sara.

"This is a beautiful house," Savannah said.

"Thank you," Kurt felt so much pride. "We just finished the work and I'm proud of it."

"All this work with those hands of yours," she teased. Savannah attempted to sound as sultry as possible. She really liked Kurt's closeness.

"Yes." Kurt lifted his hands. "Although Clint did help. So did a few of our other friends."

"Still," Savannah said. "I like a man who knows how to use his hands."

Kurt grinned. He opened the patio door and ushered her inside the bright kitchen. Savannah peered around. He'd put a lot of work into making an old house modern. She leaned against the counter as he strolled past. Savannah glanced down at his fine ass while he walked.

"Beer, wine, water or soda?" he asked.

"Beer, please."

He grabbed two bottles and slowly turned back to her. She let her gaze travel up and down his body, taking in his wide shoulders and muscular chest. His legs were long and if the bulge behind his zipper was any indication, he was stacked in every way. She licked her lips as he returned to her side.

He twisted off the top of her beer before handing it to her. Their fingers touched around the cold glass and her breath caught. She had no idea why her attraction to Kurt had hit her so hard, but she really wanted to get more than just their fingertips touching. She hadn't been seeing anyone when she'd moved back to town. In fact, it had been over a year since she'd even been on a date. After graduating from the police academy, she had concentrated on her job. She'd enjoyed patrolling her district, getting to know the residents, and was always happy when she was able to help.

If it hadn't been for Sheriff Webb calling her and telling her about the problems back here, she wouldn't have ever considered leaving. But when she'd found out about the Church and the threat to Sara and her boyfriend, she'd known she needed to come home. She'd given her notice, accepted the position of deputy and made the long drive back to town.

She hadn't had to deal with shifters yet and hadn't run into any that she knew of. Sara had told her that Clint was a wolf shifter so she was almost certain that Kurt was too.

Both of their hands were still grasping the bottle. She moved closer and had to tilt her head back to meet his gaze. There was power there. She shivered in arousal. He grinned and leaned closer.

Her eyes fluttered closed as his mouth lowered toward hers.

"So, let me ask you a question," Kurt murmured.

"You can ask me whatever you want," Savannah told him.

"What are you doing Friday night?"

Savannah leaned in closer. "No plans."

"How about I take you to the new steak house in town?" Kurt asked. "We'll have a nice dinner then take a stroll under the moon."

"That sounds good." Savannah couldn't believe her luck. Her first day back and she'd already met the hottest guy in town.

"I should probably warn you that I work with the wolf shifter Council. Just in case you didn't know that about me."

Savannah nodded. "I guessed that. Sara told me about Clint and Sheriff Webb told me about the trouble here."

"And you're okay with it?"

"I have to confess that I've never met a shifter." She grinned. "That I know of. With you all just coming out, there's always a chance that I didn't know."

"You're correct," Kurt agreed.

Savannah needed to think about how fast things were moving.

"There's time before Friday. I'll give you my number and if you change your mind, just text me. No hard feelings."

"Sure." But Savannah didn't want to change her mind. She gripped the front of Kurt's shirt to pull him the remaining distance. "But maybe we could skip to the good-night kiss just to make sure we should have that dinner."

Kurt pressed his lips to hers. She felt that same jolt that had been there when they'd touched. Savannah moaned, opening her mouth to accept his tongue.

"Food's ready!" Sara called, walking into the kitchen.

Savannah jumped away from Kurt and looked over to her friend.

Sara's eyes were wide. "Oh, shit! Sorry!"

Kurt just chuckled and backed away farther. "Shall we get something to eat? A pre-date dinner maybe?"

Disappointed, Savannah followed him out back. Hopefully she'd get another chance to feel his lips against hers. Sara was already out the door, leaving Savannah to watch Kurt's ass as he strolled in front of her.

"I can feel you staring at my ass," he said, glancing behind him.

"Well, you'd better feed me so I don't take a bite out of you."

Chapter One

Kurt had the latest reports spread out in front of him, covering every inch of his desk. The Council had provided the information he needed, but it was up to him and Clint to sort through what would help them shut down Dan Carter and his churches once and for all.

"Five chapters," Clint murmured.

Kurt glanced up at him before darting a look over to the map they'd placed on one wall. The five locations of the Church for Humanity were marked with big red Xs.

Kurt was certain the entire Church was still up to no good, and with law enforcement's hands being tied, Kurt had to watch out for his own people. The police couldn't go after anyone without proof, but Kurt didn't have the same restrictions. His entire mission was to end the Church's threat to the shifters by any means necessary.

"California, Arizona, Texas, Missouri and Louisiana." Clint stood to pace in front of the map. "Why those states? What are they up to?"

Kurt knew his friend was frustrated. Hell, they all were. He leaned back in his chair. "Those are the states with the biggest public Packs," he supplied.

Clint shook his head. "Even so... There's something..."

The shifters around the world had worked with their governments and leaders to announce their existence. The purpose for this was to ensure that even in their animal forms, they were protected. Too many shifters lost their lives each year after being hunted.

No Pack was made to go public. Each Alpha had the choice — become public or stay hidden. About sixty-five percent had chosen to become public.

The Council had known there would be some outside resistance. But Dan Carter and the Church he'd started were more than just the usual threat. They were organized and wanted the shifters gone.

Clint snapped his fingers. "Those five states are the ones that had the most opposition from their state representatives on shifters! I remember watching a special on it with Sara."

Kurt jerked in his seat and looked back at the map. He thought back to when they'd first come out. *Damn, Clint's right.* "You watch stuff like that with Sara?"

"She wants to know everything she can," Clint said. "She told me it's now her fight, too."

Kurt smiled. Clint had chosen the perfect woman for him. "So, what's this mean? Carter has the backing of some powerful people? That would not be good for us."

"I don't know, but I think it's a possibility. A scary one."

When the government had gone to the Senate and House about the reveal of the shifters, several members of those five states had opposed shifter protection laws. A few had even wanted the shifters gathered up and imprisoned. Kurt stood beside Clint. "They're getting help from somewhere, so this makes sense," he stated in disbelief. "The Church does have more powerful people behind them than we first thought."

Clint nodded.

"Which means that if word gets out that Colt is there undercover, he could be in even more danger," Kurt said.

"Shit, I didn't think about that. We need to look at who knows about Colt's work."

"We need to call Tony and set up a meeting with the Council."

Clint nodded. "You call Alpha Babcock and I'll try to get hold of Tony."

Kurt laughed. Clint had the hardest time around the Alpha Council members. Clint's instincts were in constant battle, having to work for an entire Council full of Alphas. Most shifters only had to answer to the Alpha in charge of their Pack. The instincts that drove them were as different as their personalities. Kurt had a knack for dealing with the Council while Clint was pure hunter. It was what made them such a great team.

He walked over to the phone on his desk and dialed Council Alpha Babcock's number. Alpha Babcock was Kurt's immediate boss—a good older Alpha, a man Kurt had really come to respect and admire. Thirty years ago, he'd overseen a Pack in the wide plains of Oklahoma but had given his Pack over to his younger brother in order to join the Council.

"Hello."

"Alpha Babcock," Kurt greeted.

"How many times have I told you to call me Tim?" Alpha Babcock asked with a laugh.

"Sorry, sir." It was ingrained in him to show respect to any Alpha. He just couldn't help it.

Alpha Babcock just sighed. "Fine. What have you got?"

"I think Clint and I have found something. Is there any way you and Alpha Conrad could swing by my office?"

"We were just breaking for dinner. Give us fifteen minutes and we'll be there."

"That would be great," he responded.

"See you soon."

The Alpha hung up the phone and Kurt glanced at Clint. "Tony will be here too," Clint said.

"The Alphas are on their way," Kurt told his friend.

Clint snorted. "Great."

"Just Babcock and Conrad. I'm glad Tony is still staying here. I'd hate to have to tell him this over the phone."

Tony, the face of the Packs, had been instrumental in the shifters coming out. He'd been staying at the Council compound since the issues had come up with the Church. Tony was also the contact between several shifter species and the Council. Kurt, Clint and Tony had become fast friends. It wasn't well known, either, that the undercover shifter inside Carter's church was in some sort of relationship with Tony as well.

"Yeah," Clint said. "You need me to stay?"

"You connected the dots," Kurt praised. "I think I can handle two Alphas."

Clint grunted. "Fine."

"I'll owe you," Kurt said.

"After, I want to go into town and see Sara," Clint demanded. There was a lightness in his eyes when he spoke about Sara. Kurt couldn't deny him.

"We can do that," Kurt agreed.

"Great!" Clint said before he smirked. "I think Deputy Conley was going to stop by."

Kurt flinched. He couldn't control the action and Clint's chuckle told him his friend hadn't missed it. He'd sort of been avoiding Savannah... Okay, he was avoiding her. They'd connected the night they'd met, but afterward he'd been spooked by such an intense link. She'd been receptive. Hell, they'd been ready for more than just the passionate kiss they'd almost shared.

It was only after he'd left that night that his brain had caught up with his hard dick. He'd been feeling sorry for himself.

He'd been the one to cancel the date.

Everyone around him had started to settle down and he'd been panicking. That did not mean he was ready to give up his freedoms as a single man. Sure, every time he thought about the sexy blonde Savannah Conley, his cock filled and his wolf wanted to claim her.

But, damn it, he wasn't ready! So, he'd been avoiding the woman for several weeks. Clint took way too much pleasure in teasing him. Clint had every reason to mess with him about it, since Kurt had been kind of mean when it came to Clint's courting of Sara. Or lack of courting....

"I'm not interested in her," Kurt told his friend.

"That's not what Sara said she witnessed," Clint taunted.

"Sara needs a hobby."

"Oh, I keep her plenty busy," Clint responded.

"I think I need to assign you more work," Kurt griped. It was too late to try to get out of going into town. He was going to have to buck up and see Savannah.

"You have to come with me. Sara wants to talk to you about Thanksgiving dinner." Clint just grinned, rocking back on the heels of his feet.

"Thanksgiving," Kurt repeated. He'd already promised to not only attend but to bring something. It was the first holiday that Sara was hosting with Clint. She was so excited and he couldn't let her down.

"I don't like you anymore."

Clint laughed. Luckily, a knock on the door interrupted any further taunts Clint had in store for him.

Kurt motioned to Clint. "Get the damn door."

Clint winked, but he did stroll to the door and pulled it open. Both Alphas stood on the threshold, along with Tony.

"Come in, please," Kurt called out.

When the Alphas and Tony entered his office, Kurt realized that he should have cleaned up a little. His papers were still scattered around and it looked like a hurricane had come through.

"I see you've been busy," Alpha Babcock commented.

"Yes, and you're not going to like what we found."

"That's what we suspected," Alpha Conrad said.

"Please sit down." Kurt motioned toward the small sitting area. "Does anyone want coffee?"

"No, thank you," Babcock answered.

The small area set to the side had a couch and a couple of chairs. Kurt sat in one chair and Tony took the other. The Alphas settled onto the couch.

"What's going on?" Tony asked.

Clint leaned against the counter behind Tony's shoulder. Kurt could see the compassion on his best friend's face.

"Who knows about Colt?" Kurt asked. It was the question that had the most serious consequences.

"Why?" Tony demanded.

Clint stepped forward and placed his palm on Tony's shoulder.

"We linked Dan Carter's churches to the states that had the most opposition on the shifters coming out," Kurt said. "I think, with a little more digging, we'll learn that some of government is aiding Carter."

Tony paled.

"Would anyone know about Colt's undercover work?" Kurt asked.

"No," Tony said. "The Council and my Pack. No one in the government."

"That's good. We need to keep it that way," Kurt said.

"Tell us what you know and how we can help," Babcock said.

* * * *

Savannah pushed open the door to the Blend and Brew coffee shop. The aroma of the strong beans that Sara used was mouthwatering. Her friend glanced up from behind the counter and smiled wide. Savannah nodded and greeted other customers as she made her way to the counter. Sara was wiping down the work surface when Savannah finally reached her.

"Surprise me," she told her friend.

Sara's entire face lit up. Savannah knew that Sara continually worked on blends and loved experimenting with flavors. The pleasure Sara showed at Savannah's simple request was worth a pot of gold.

Savannah had really missed her friend. She made it a point of stopping by every day so that she could reconnect with Sara. She was thrilled to see how happy

Sara was. Sara had found the love of her life and owned the business she'd always wanted.

Thinking of Sara's boyfriend brought Savannah's thoughts to Kurt Moore. The handsome man she'd met at Sara's house haunted her dreams. Okay, maybe not just at night. She found herself constantly looking for him when she was out on patrol, hoping to get another glance at him.

Since that day, he'd avoided all contact. He was running from her. She'd asked Sara about it, but her friend had been just confused as she was. If Clint knew anything, he was keeping it to himself.

He just told Savannah that Kurt was interested and would come around.

Sara was humming as she worked the espresso machine. Before long she handed Savannah a paper cup of the most tantalizing brew.

Savannah blew on the hot drink before taking a sip. Cinnamon exploded on her tongue and she moaned.

Sara beamed at her.

"This is amazing," Savannah told her sincerely.

"Thanks!" Sara responded happily. "It's my holiday special blend."

Thanksgiving was less than a week away and Savannah thought Sara's new coffee blend would go perfectly with a nice traditional Thanksgiving dinner.

"You're still coming to our house Thursday, right?" Sara asked.

Savannah nodded. "I'll be there with my green bean casserole and cranberry sauce," she promised.

Savannah's family had moved away after she had gone to college in Arizona. Her parents now lived in Florida and her brother in New York. She was grateful that Sara had thought to invite her to spend Thanksgiving Day with them.

The front door of the shop opened and Savannah stepped away from the counter to give the new customers room. She sat at one of the tables to enjoy her hot drink. Her shift didn't start for another thirty minutes so she would easily be able to make it to the station in time.

A slight frost clung to the trees and sidewalks. Winter had arrived but the weather was still considered mild. Savannah knew that wouldn't last long. The entire sheriff's department was working these next few days to make sure that the residents and town were prepared for the winter storm headed their way from Canada.

Since she was scheduled to drive to the outskirts of town to make sure the residents knew about the storm and had everything they needed, she knew she would be feeling the chill all day. She'd have to take some of Sara's new blend with her.

She was still sipping her coffee, just enjoying the cozy interior of the shop, when the door opened once again. She lifted her gaze and locked on Kurt as he stepped through. He darted a look around the room before landing on her.

She smiled and lifted her cup to him in greeting. He nodded even as he took a step away. Clint, who was at Kurt's back, kept him from moving more than a foot. Clint said something into Kurt's ear before pushing Kurt in her direction.

Savannah lifted an eyebrow, amused by their interaction. Kurt shuffled toward her. If Savannah didn't truly believe he was interested in her she would have been insulted. Instead she trusted her gut when it came to Kurt Moore. Attraction and interest showed plainly in the depth of his gaze. Whether he was relationship-shy or something else was yet to be seen.

However, Savannah was not going to give up on him.

"Hi," he said when he reached her.

She smiled up at him. "Hey, Kurt, it's good to see you."

He nodded and shifted his feet.

"Will you join me?" she asked.

He glanced over his shoulder toward the counter. Clint and Sara were both leaning over the wide barrier, kissing. "Clint's supposed to be grabbing me a cup," he said before sitting across from her.

Savannah laughed. "It might be a few minutes then."

Kurt snorted and rolled his eyes. "Tell me about it. They're already kissing, aren't they?"

"Yep."

He leaned back in his chair before stretching his legs out. To Savannah, it appeared he was trying too hard to act casual. She was more than a little amused by the performance.

"So how have you been? I haven't seen you much."

Kurt pressed his lips together. "Yeah, I meant... I wanted to... I've been busy at work."

Savannah was intrigued by the man stumbling over his words. He had been so confident before.

Kurt shook his head and cursed. "I've been busy with a project."

"You're still looking into the Church?" she questioned, keeping her voice low so they wouldn't be overheard. She hadn't been there when the Church had first arrived in town, but since she'd started working, they got weekly updates about it. Sheriff Webb wanted to make sure that all his deputies were on constant guard against trouble.

Not only was his daughter involved with the shifter the Church had kidnapped, but one of his own deputies had been implicated in the crime. It had hit Sheriff

Webb hard. He wasn't going to allow any more trouble in his town.

"Yeah." Kurt leaned back in his chair and seemed more relaxed discussing the threat than anything personal between them.

If that helped Kurt open up to her, she was all for that.

"I think we might have a connection as to why the chapters are popping up where they are," Kurt told her.

"That's great."

"I hope we can get to the bottom of this before there is any more danger to the Packs."

"We will," Clint said confidently as he joined them. He passed Kurt a cup of coffee before he sat down.

"That's good news. I know Sheriff Webb has been uneasy not knowing what the church is truly up to."

"After we know more, I'll need to set up another meeting with him," Kurt continued. "We have a few people gathering more intel, but I think we're on the right track."

Savannah's watch beeped and she glanced at it. She sighed, hating to have to leave in the middle of her conversation with Kurt when he'd finally settled.

"I have to get to the station," she told the guys before standing.

Kurt looked disappointed for a minute before clearing his features.

"Oh! Kurt, Sara wanted me to make sure you were still bringing the salad on Thursday," Clint said as if he had just remembered.

"I said I would," Kurt replied with a frown.

Clint winked discreetly at Savannah. She had to press her lips firmly together to keep from smiling. Clint had just to make sure she knew that she would see Kurt in a few days.

"I'm going to get a refill and I'll catch up with you boys later," she told them.

Kurt grunted suddenly right after she heard a sound under the table. She was pretty sure Clint had just kicked him. Kurt moved his coffee from one hand to the other before standing. "I'll walk you out."

Pleased, she nodded.

She passed the counter and Sara gave her another cup while taking the empty one from her hand. Sara must have been watching since she had one ready for her. Savannah thanked her friend, glad they wouldn't have to wait and Kurt couldn't sneak off again.

Kurt placed his hand on the small of her back as they walked across the floor. Even through her uniform and the thickness of her coat, she could still feel the warmth of his touch.

She'd begun to crave him, thinking about how his hands would feel caressing her body while they made love. Her face heated and she had to clear her suddenly dry throat.

She thanked him softly when he opened the door for her, letting her slip out first. The cold blast of wind shocked her and her eyes began to water. Kurt wrapped his arm around her waist as he escorted her to the SUV she'd parked in front of the shop.

"It was good to see you," she said to him when they reached her vehicle.

Kurt moved in front of her. "I'm sorry I've been acting so weird. I just didn't expect..." He waved his hand between the two of them.

Savannah wrapped her free hand around the lapel of Kurt's jacket. "What's changed? I don't want to force you into anything."

Kurt grinned. "You're not. A buddy of mine said some things that made sense. I realized that if I kept my head up my ass, I might lose the chance to get to know you better," he admitted.

Savannah lifted to her toes and pressed her lips gently against his. "Tell this buddy I said thank you."

"Yeah, I'll have to do that," he replied before kissing her more deeply.

Their tongues met in desperation and she moaned. Kurt tasted so good—coffee and something manly and wild. She had wondered about the kiss she'd not gotten before. And now she knew.

Oh boy, did she know. His hold was firm but gentle. His mouth moved slowly, his tongue talented as he lapped at her. Her shiver was not from the cold.

He licked at her lips before pulling back. "You better get to work."

She dropped her head back and groaned. "Damn it."

Kurt took a step back. "I'm guessing from Clint's so obvious mention of Thanksgiving that I'll see you at Sara and Clint's on Thursday?"

She laughed. "Caught that, did you? Yes, I'll be there."

"Good." He reached over, opened the car door and held on to it while she climbed inside. "See you soon."

* * * *

Kurt rubbed his eyes, growing more and more tired. It was after two in the morning and he'd finally stepped away from looking into Dan Carter and his Church's connection to the politicians of the five key states. They had to have proof of wrongdoing and conspiracy against the shifters to take to the authorities. They couldn't accuse high members of Congress without absolute evidence.

He had pictures of the congressmen from Texas and Missouri meeting with Dan Carter. That might be explained away, but the fact that their meeting had been just days before the kidnapping in Riverwood was suspicious.

The shifter who was currently undercover with the Church had also confirmed that he'd seen the Governor of Arizona at one of the gatherings before the Church had invaded Lovington.

The pieces were starting to come together, but Kurt still worried about what plans Dan Carter and the others had. Dan Carter hadn't been seen since the kidnapping in Riverwood had been foiled.

Riverwood, Kurt's home Pack, had been plagued with devastating fires that had almost destroyed the town. He and Clint and a few of their closest friends had gone to help.

While rescuing his brother's mate Todd, Kurt had gotten his first and only look at Dan Carter, when the man had visited the house where Todd had been held. Right after that, Dan Carter had disappeared.

Even with everything Kurt had managed to put together, there was just no information on Dan Carter. Carter had sent his second-in-command, Perry Costa, up to Lovington but had never appeared himself. And Perry had been the person responsible for Clint's kidnapping.

When the shifters had announced their presence, the Council, through Tony, had also shared details with the public. Myths had been debunked for the protection of the shifters. A bite for a scratch from a shifter didn't turn a person into one. Shifters did not transform during the full moon. Shifters did not hunt down humans to eat them.

Still, there were many people who did not understand, didn't want to get to know the shifters. Friends he'd known for years had turned their backs on him and Clint as soon as they'd found out what they truly were.

They'd been born different. And Kurt loved the ability to shift. He wouldn't change one thing about being able to transform. He didn't know any shifter who would.

Tony had been dealing with the questions longer than anyone. Tony had even confessed to Kurt that some of the more common questions were just foolish beliefs that had been passed down over the years. Tony's main job back then had been to represent the wolves so that humans who were afraid could have someone to look at and understand that they were just humans with a unique gift.

Kurt still remembered watching Tony standing proud in front of the cameras answering one foolish question after another. If it had been him, he would have told the stupid reporters exactly what he thought of them and their inquiries. Tony, however, had handled it with class.

Thinking about the man brought to mind the conversation the two of them had shared days ago. Clint had been teasing him once again about Savannah, and when his friend had gone to check on a few things, Tony had brought the subject up.

Kurt had suspected that Tony was regretting Colt taking the undercover assignment. Tony walked around in misery until he got a rare call from Colt. Whenever Colt called in information or Tony spoke about the other man, Tony's entire demeanor changed. His face lit up and came alive at the mention of Colt.

So, when Tony had cornered Kurt and asked why he was running from his possible mate, Kurt had confided in the man. He wasn't sure if the instant longing for Savannah was because of her, or if it was a product of the people closest to him finding their own mates.

He'd tried to convince himself he liked being a bachelor, but it had been a lie. He didn't — he wanted someone to come home to every night. He'd spent weeks talking himself into fighting what deep down he really knew. He wanted Savannah. He just wasn't sure why.

And that was what had really been bothering him.

Tony had given him some sage advice. There was only one way to find out — man up and spend some time getting to know Savannah. If what he felt so strongly was still there, then he needed to step up and decide what to do.

One look at Savannah that day in the coffee shop and Kurt had known that Tony was right. He'd been flustered at first and that initial reaction had shocked him. He'd never been tongue-tied before in his life. Luckily, she hadn't called him an idiot and taken off. He'd gotten his act together and they had managed a decent conversation before she'd had to go into work.

The kiss they'd shared in the cold morning air had heated him plenty. His cock hardened at just the memory of her lips against his, her soft body wrapped tight in his arms.

He dropped his hand to his lap and rubbed. Oh yeah, he couldn't wait to see her in a few days at Clint and Sara's Thanksgiving dinner.

Now that he'd decided to wrap his head around starting a relationship with Savannah, his body and the wolf part of him wanted to hurry.

Kurt unsnapped his jeans and fished his erection out. He was already hard and leaking just thinking about Savannah. He stroked himself firmly, thinking about what he wanted to do with her. He wondered what her mouth would feel like wrapped around his shaft. He ran his thumb over the head of his hardon, gathering up the liquid. He craved the feel of her hand on him just like this. He pumped faster, longing to bury himself deep inside her wet pussy. He moaned at that thought, his cock straining in his hold. He wanted to lose himself inside her.

Savannah's soft skin under his hands would feel nice.

Kurt closed his eyes.

Would she cry out softly or scream for him? God, Kurt wanted to know the answer to that.

His hips snapped up and finally, with the picture of Savannah under his hard body, he came. He milked his cock until he was completely spent then relaxed back into his office chair and grinned. If he could come so hard from just fantasizing about being with Savannah, the actual act might just bring him to his knees.

He couldn't wait.

Kurt stood up before walking over to the small sink by the sitting area. He needed to go home. He had a nice big house that he should be in. Not stuck in his office inside the Council compound.

He cleaned up before fixing his pants. Once he was presentable, he headed toward the door. Kurt hoped he could avoid seeing anyone around the place for the moment. All he wanted to do was sit in his new leather recliner and kick back with a beer, maybe fantasize about Savannah a little more.

The hall was quiet as he made his way to the front door. He passed one guard and nodded to the young shifter before opening the front door. He'd parked his truck close to the building so he ran to his vehicle. It was colder that he'd expected. If Kurt had to guess, he'd have said that the cold front was moving in faster than the weatherman had claimed.

Damn. He hit the key fob to unlock the door.

After climbing inside, Kurt turned on the truck before moving the heater to full blast. He sat and rubbed his hands together to ward off the cold.

Savannah was out working in this weather.

If he knew where Savannah was, he'd take her a hot coffee or something.

Instead he put his truck in gear and backed out of his parking spot. There was a little moisture on the ground but luckily no ice. Still, he drove carefully the entire way home.

When he pulled up in front of his house, he was glad that he'd left the front porch and living room light on. At least he wasn't coming home to darkness. He parked under the cover he and Clint had built and turned off the truck.

Maybe one day he would be coming home after a long day and be greeted by someone who loved him. It might not be Savannah, but it could be. Kurt just needed to be open to the possibility. Maybe Savannah wasn't the one.

But what if she was…

He had to find out. Kurt was tired of being alone, but he wouldn't settle for anything less than true love.

Kurt turned off his truck. The cold immediately filled the cab.

He hated winter.

It was going to be a cold, lonely night. *Maybe I should get a dog.*

Chapter Two

Savannah stepped into her shower stall and sighed with relief as the hot water flowed over her. The expected cold front had hit hard and she was frozen to the bone. Even having the heater on in her vehicle while patrolling hadn't seemed to be enough as she'd had to keep getting out and talking to people.

Normally, she enjoyed checking on residents at the edge of town like she'd been doing the last couple of nights. She had reconnected with several people whom she had grown up with. But on a cold night like tonight, she was just exhausted. Tired, cold and miserable.

She'd made it a point to visit every house to make sure they had plenty of firewood and gas, wanting to be sure the residents of her town would be okay if they lost power. She'd checked generators and taken count of numbers of family members, just in case.

On her way back home, she'd driven by the big compound that the shifters resided in. She'd checked in at the gate and had been assured they were prepared for anything Mother Nature brought them. She knew that Kurt had recently moved out of the compound and into a house close to Sara's, but Savannah had been hoping for a glimpse of him. No such luck. She'd driven back to her own house thinking about the handsome shifter.

But she would be seeing him the next afternoon when they had Thanksgiving dinner over at Sara and Clint's, though, so she did have something to look forward to. She hoped to find a little alone time with Kurt sometime soon.

With the water pounding at the sore muscles of her neck, Savannah picked up her scented shower gel and poured a liberal amount onto her shoulders and chest. She rubbed the vanilla-scented soap into her body before closing her eyes and leaning back against the shower wall.

Truth be told, she'd been spending too much time fantasizing about Kurt when she was in the shower, driving or lying in bed. Okay, she was constantly thinking about having Kurt buried inside her and the two of them going at it. Sex was a great stress reliever. Sex with Kurt? That, she knew, would be earth-shattering.

Thinking of Kurt's touch instead of her own, she ran her hands around her breasts to pull at her nipples. The result was a zing that traveled to her core. She followed the feeling with her fingers to tease at her clit. She rubbed, lifted one leg up, playing with herself.

Oh, that's good.

She hummed, pressing harder against the little nub. She wanted Kurt's hands on her like this. God, how she wanted him!

Savannah braced one foot against the wall as she slipped her hand lower and fingered her folds. The tip of her finger entered her pussy easily. She pushed in deeper.

It had been a while since she'd had a lover. And her fingers were no substitute for a nice, hard cock.

Adding a second finger, she pumped deeply and rocked her hips. She lowered her other hand and played with her clit again. Her breathing picked up and her cunt tingled.

She climaxed with a small moan. The release was nice, but nowhere close to what she was really craving.

Savannah removed her fingers from her pussy and picked the shower gel up. She gave her body a quick wash. At least she felt warmer. Rinsing off, she smiled, thinking about Kurt showering with her the next time.

She had to get up early to make sure that her two promised dishes would be ready to take to Sara's. Sara had told her that she'd given Kurt the job of bringing the salad since he was, after all, a man. Savannah had laughed at that. It was just another thing she needed to learn about the man she was interested in. Did he like to cook? If he didn't, she could teach him a few easy but good meals.

Most of the information she did know about him, she had gotten from Sara and Clint. But she wanted to know him, to find out what made him tick. There was only so much a person could learn about someone without really spending time with them.

She wanted to know all the little things that made Kurt so fascinating.

She turned off the water and reached blindly for the towel she'd hung over the shower rod. She wiped the water from her face, wondering about his habits. Did he prefer to shower in the morning or at night? Did he like to curl up on the couch and watch movies or was he more of a book person? Was he an early riser or did he like to sleep in?

Those were things she wanted to find out by experiencing them with him.

She would start working on finding the answers the next day.

After wiping off the excess water from her body, Savannah wrapped the towel around her. The bedroom lamp was dimly lit in the corner of the bedroom as she stepped from the bathroom to her room. She still had boxes stacked up against one wall. Since she had gone straight to work, Savannah hadn't had the time to unpack. She wasn't even sure how long she'd be in the small rental house.

The family who'd once lived in the home had been happy to rent it out for a small fee. Luckily for Savannah, all the utilities were still on. Sheriff Webb had planned on whoever the deputy was staying there, so Savannah was fortunate enough not to have to bunk with someone else. Although Sara had offered her a spare room, Savannah didn't want to put her friend out when Clint had just moved in.

Plus, Savannah enjoyed having her own space. She'd lived on her own for too long to have roommates.

Not unless there was a sexy shifter in her bed.

At least for a couple nights.

She wasn't planning on living with Kurt any time soon, but some sleepovers with him would be great.

Instead of dressing, Savannah tossed the towel onto a chair before climbing underneath the heavy gray comforter on her bed. She'd skipped dinner, but she was too exhausted to even think about cooking.

Burying herself under the mound of blankets, she peered over to the empty side of the bed. Maybe, just maybe, it wouldn't be empty for long.

Savannah smiled before closing her eyes and letting herself begin to drift off to sleep.

* * * *

Kurt knew Sara had given him the easiest assignment of food for the dinner—a salad for eight. Not that difficult to do. He'd picked up the ingredients earlier in the week. He could have bought a pre-made salad—in fact Sara had probably thought he would—but he wanted to surprise her. She had, after all, been giving him a hard time about not being able to cook.

But he would show her. He had his laptop open on the counter with the web page that he had saved. He'd googled simple, easy salad recipes and had found one that even he couldn't screw up. Not that he was trying to impress anyone...

Oh hell, who was he kidding? He wanted to impress Savannah. And if he pleased Sara with his contribution to dinner, she was sure to share that with her friend.

He'd already showered and dressed in his best pair of jeans and a dark blue long-sleeved Henley. After he finished putting his ingredients together, he would be ready to go. He chopped up the iceberg lettuce then added it to the romaine he already had in the bowl.

Kurt had about half an hour before he needed to leave for Clint's. Living just a couple of blocks away would be convenient since a snow storm had hit the night before. The first snowfall of year had come with two solid inches. Even now there were still small flurries falling. He hoped the roads weren't bad. Since there hadn't been time for the snow to melt and freeze again, he didn't think they would be too dangerous and he really wanted Savannah to make it over for dinner.

Kurt finished the last of the lettuce before lining up the carrots to slice. He worked quickly until he had all the ingredients inside the large plastic bowl he'd purchased. He snapped the lid closed before tossing it up in the air and catching it easily. It was a tossed salad, after all.

Laughing at himself, he set the bowl to the side and headed into the back of the house to get his boots and jacket. He paused by the front door and picked up his keys from the side table. He pressed the remote start and, hearing the two beeps, pocketed his keys.

The hall down to his bedroom had been painted tan and a few pictures hung neatly on the wall. The majority of the pictures were of his unit in the Army. They'd served together for eight years and he missed his men. Clint was the only one he saw daily. The other members of his elite unit had spread out and gone their separate ways. They still kept in touch, but as time went by, the calls were becoming less and less frequent.

It was just another big change in his life.

He paused in front of the last photo — the most recent. This picture was of his younger brother, Kenny, and Kenny's mate, Todd, the scene captured right after the two men had performed their mating ceremony. It had been a proud moment for Kurt to witness.

He wished Kenny and Todd had been able to come up for the day or long weekend, but Kenny was still training Mike Jackson to take over his position with the Pack. Kurt understood that his brother couldn't make it, even if he was disappointed. He wanted his brother to meet Savannah and Savannah to get to know his family. Christmas was just around the corner, though, and Kenny had promised to visit for that holiday.

Kurt continued back to his bedroom that he'd decorated for comfort. The dark walls mixed nicely with his dark wood furniture. He didn't have photos on his bedroom walls but instead had purchased a large mural for the wall over his bed.

The art showcased a pack of wolves standing tall at the top of a hill. The artist had captured the sunset and the wolves looked strong and protective. He'd seen the mural for sale on the Internet and had just had to have it. It was the first large purchase he'd made for his new home.

He grabbed a pair of socks from his drawer before picking up his boots from the end of the bed. He finished dressing quickly and headed out. He slung on his winter jacket before picking up his salad bowl.

One last look around to make sure that everything was in place and he was out of the door. His walkway wasn't icy, but his boots crunched over the crisp snow. His truck heater warmed him as he opened the door and climbed inside. He appreciated the technology of the remote start. Not having to go outside in the winter to warm up the vehicle was fantastic.

He carefully pulled out of his drive and started toward his best friend's house.

The drive to Clint and Sara's was quiet. The streets were empty and the untouched snow that blanketed the town was gorgeous.

Several cars were already in the drive when he arrived. He recognized Savannah's SUV and Ryan's truck. Ryan was one of the guards at the Council compound and he was dating Sara's assistant at the coffee shop, Cecil. Kurt liked both men and was glad to see they were joining them.

He parked behind Savannah and shut off his truck. He took a deep breath, grabbed the salad then hurried up to the front door. He knocked and the door was opened immediately by Clint.

"Good, you're here," Clint greeted and pulled him into a hug.

Kurt returned the embrace before pulling back and holding up his container. "And with food."

Both men laughed. Clint closed the door and swung his arm around his shoulders, leading him away from the entry. "We're hanging in the kitchen. Sara's dad got a call about a small fender bender so she wants to wait for him before we eat."

Clint caught the happy sound of conversation just before he entered the kitchen. Sara and Savannah were behind the kitchen island, covering the serving dishes with foil. Ryan sat at one of the bar stools with Cecil standing between his legs. Ryan lifted a beer to Kurt and Cecil gave him a small wave. Sara came around the counter to take the salad and gave him a quick hug.

He gave everyone a greeting, but his gaze was really locked on the other woman in the room. Savannah wore a pair of snug black pants and a bright red sweater, and her silky long blonde hair cascaded down her back. She looked absolutely beautiful. She smiled at him then followed Sara's lead and gave him a hug.

He slipped his arm around her waist and held on. "Happy Thanksgiving," he murmured quietly.

"Happy Thanksgiving to you," she responded, easily fitting in his embrace.

Clint opened the fridge and held out a bottle of beer in question. Kurt nodded. There was nothing better than a nice cold beer while gathering with friends. Clint popped the top off before he slid the bottle over to him. Kurt caught it and took a long pull.

Savannah and Sara were sipping on glasses of wine, talking about old friends from their school days. Ryan was teasing Cecil about his cooking. Kurt glanced up and met Clint's gaze.

Clint was grinning at him. Clint peered from Kurt to Savannah then back to him. Clint's eyebrow lifted in question.

Kurt just shrugged in response and ran his fingers up and down Savannah's side. If she was accepting his touch, he would not complain about it. Yes, it was a change from only a few short days ago, but Kurt was taking Tony's advice to heart. Tony was having to live with Colt working undercover and couldn't be with him. Kurt was lucky that Savannah was within arms' reach.

Clint nodded in acceptance.

That few seconds of silent communication warmed Kurt. In his own way, he had claimed Savannah and Clint accepted her as part of them. Kurt knew that Clint would look to protect Savannah at all costs, as Kurt would do with Sara. That was what they did for each other—looked out for each other and their loved ones.

A knock at the door had conversation halting around the island.

"That's probably Tony," Clint said, placing his beer on the counter. "I invited him to join us."

Clint left the room, and Savannah looked up at Kurt. "Did you find anything else on the Church?"

"A little," he admitted. "We have enough to draw a connection to all the parties, but we still don't know the end game."

Tony joined them in the kitchen. The stress and worry on his face were obvious.

"Everything okay?" Kurt asked his friend.

Tony nodded but didn't look too sure. "Colt missed his check-in. I hate when that happens."

"How long?" Clint questioned, coming up behind Tony.

"He was supposed to call last night," Tony informed them.

It was a little before noon now. Kurt frowned. "When was the last time you spoke to him?"

"Three days ago." Tony accepted a bottle of beer from Clint. "He's missed check-ins before, but never this long. There's probably nothing to worry about. He knows to get out if he thinks there's an immediate threat on his life. There will always be some kind of danger, but he needs to survive this assignment."

Tony spoke quietly and Kurt wanted to reach out and offer him some support. What Tony was going through couldn't be easy. "If you need anything at all, you let me know," Kurt told him.

Tony smiled. "I will. But let's not think about it right now. Colt can take care of himself and I don't want to ruin anyone's holiday."

"You're not ruining anything," Sara assured him. "But if we don't eat soon, the food won't be as good. We should go ahead and eat. I'll make my dad a plate when he comes back."

Sara and Savannah instructed the men where to put dishes. The kitchen table had been pulled away from the wall and a leaf had been added to make the seating fit eight people instead of four.

The table had already been set and, after the food was arranged, they took their seats. Kurt was pleased when

Savannah sat between him and Tony. He liked having her so close and knew he didn't have to worry about Tony hitting on her.

Food began to be passed around the table and Kurt filled his plate with turkey, stuffing, sweet potatoes, salad, casserole and cranberry sauce. He looked at his overflowing dish and grinned.

Savannah elbowed him. "What are you smiling about?"

Kurt chuckled. "I was just thinking about last Thanksgiving." Clint snorted next to him.

"Oh?" Savannah inquired.

"We were chasing a rogue in South America," Kurt said, still laughing.

"Fucking MREs," Clint grumbled.

"What are MREs?" Cecil asked. He looked between Kurt and Clint.

"Meals ready to eat," Kurt supplied. "Basically, the worst shit in the world. Packaged up for years and we add water and eat them. Sometimes we have a fire to at least warm up the food, but not all the time."

"That's just wrong!" Savannah exclaimed.

Kurt stabbed a piece of turkey. "Yeah, and the company wasn't as good."

"That little shit was psycho," Clint added. "We caught up to him the day before Thanksgiving and couldn't get a flight back until Friday."

"I thought Clint was going to skin and roast the little pissant," Kurt continued, still laughing.

"Thought about it," Clint admitted. "Would have been better than the MREs we ate."

Everyone around the table laughed.

He'd really missed family gatherings during the holidays. He hadn't had much downtime and looked forward to more celebrations like this.

He looked over at Savannah, knowing he wanted to spend them with her as well as everyone else.

The people at the table were slowly taking the place of his birth family. Kurt wouldn't be leaving anytime soon. He owned his home. He was putting down roots. Hey, he could even host a holiday at his house.

Savannah leaned over, pressing against his arm. "You okay?"

Her voice was soft, but the shifters would be able to hear anyway. Still, Kurt didn't mind. "I'm really good. I forgot how nice having family around was for important days."

Savannah smiled back before peering around the table. At their friends. "You're right. I haven't looked forward to the holidays since I moved away."

"Well, this is just the beginning," Clint stated. He lifted his beer. "We have a home now. A place to call our own."

"A family of our choosing," Sara added. She leaned over and kissed Clint's cheek.

"To family," Savannah announced, holding up her wine glass.

"To family," everyone repeated.

As he clicked his bottle to Savannah's glass, he held her gaze. Kurt could picture many more dinners like this. Maybe with the sound of kids running around. Well maybe Clint's kids, because Kurt wasn't sure he was ready to go there quite yet. He set down his beer and picked his fork up. It was time to dig in.

The turkey was moist and flavorful. All the food was good. Kurt had even scooped up a spoonful of cranberry sauce because Savannah had made it.

Cecil laughed so hard, causing him to choke, that Ryan had to reach over and pat the young man's back. Kurt hadn't been joking about what he and Clint had been doing the last Thanksgiving. He hadn't thought to complain at the time. They'd been given a mission and Kurt always completed missions. Clint hadn't seemed to mind anything other than the food. A shifter could not survive on MREs. Not like a human solider. There had even been times over the years he and Clint had had no choice but to shift and hunt down their own food.

He preferred the store-bought turkey than trying to catch one with his teeth.

Savannah's elbow brushed his arm as she reached for a roll.

Yeah, the company was a definite improvement as well. Even with the sheriff missing and Tony's sad expression, Kurt was going to remember this holiday. The Council had offered him so much more than a job.

The Council had given him the chance to settle.

To start his life when many of others his age had already chosen a mate and began a family. He might be late, but Kurt was excited for his future.

Savannah was in heaven. Good food, great company and a handsome man at her side. It was one of the best holidays she'd had in a long time.

She'd been on patrol in Arizona the year before. The weather had been warm and without the calendar, she wouldn't have even known it was Thanksgiving. The snow on the ground here could be bothersome, but to

Savannah she saw it as a welcome to winter and what really started the holiday season. It also helped that the entire atmosphere of the house was warm and loving. Savannah wasn't alone this year.

Back in Arizona, she'd had friends, but having worked so much Savannah hadn't truly been close to many people. If she hadn't been on duty, she still wouldn't have had a place to go unless she traveled to see her family. Not that she hadn't met good people in Arizona. At one of her stops, a store owner she'd become friendly with had given her a Tupperware with turkey and all the fixings. So, it had turned out to be a good day. But nothing compared to this year. She'd woken that morning to the sight of snow-covered lawns and had been very pleased. She had missed the snow while she had lived in Arizona. The only season that Arizona had was summer. It was hot, always hot, and even at the end of November there was little break from the heat.

Once the food had been consumed, Sara stood to begin brewing a special blend of coffee she'd been saving. Already the strong, fragrant aroma was filling the kitchen. Savannah rose to begin to clear the table.

"Sit down," Sara ordered. "You're our guest."

She shook her head. "You just stay over there and make me some of the awesome-smelling coffee. I got this."

"Let me help too, then," Cecil said as he jumped up.

Savannah hadn't known Cecil when she'd lived there before, but she liked Sara's assistant. He was funny and sweet. Cecil was also obviously in love with Ryan. Ryan hadn't been in town much longer than Kurt and Clint.

Before the shifters had come out to the public, Savannah hadn't had any idea that they lived so close to town, or that the sheriff's department worked with them to keep both the town and the Council safe. There had been an agreement between the shifters and law enforcement for decades.

Savannah set the plates in the sink after Cecil. She went back to the table as Cecil went to help Sara.

She pressed against Kurt's arm as he spoke to Tony about Tony's brother and his mate. Tony was sharing the story about how Cain and Emily were dealing with being first-time parents.

Kurt smiled before sliding his palm down her back as she leaned over him, collecting more of the plates and silverware. It took a few trips back and forth from the table to the sink and Savannah enjoyed flirting with Kurt.

No, she might not be in high school anymore, but Kurt made her feel young and free again. She could laugh and joke with him, run up and entice him until they got the chance to be alone. Savannah didn't have plans for the rest of the night so maybe she'd even invite him over to see her new place. Although she really should have planned that idea better. Other than a few dishes, her clothes and bathroom items, she hadn't unpacked anything. It would be hard to entertain at her house. Hell, she hadn't even hooked up her TV yet.

Kurt didn't seem to mind her teasing, either.

As she passed him, Kurt's hand moved over more intimate places until he brushed over the side of her breasts. Yeah, they were on the same page, all right. With the table cleared, she sat back down beside Kurt as Sara and Cecil finished up getting the drinks. Was it her imagination or was Kurt's chair closer?

He pressed his knee against hers, and yes indeed, he'd moved one of the chairs to where they would be in very close quarters.

Cecil came back to the table and passed out cups. The aroma of the coffee wafted up and she took a deep breath. Savannah took a sip and moaned.

Sara took her seat and grinned. "Good?"

"I don't know how you do it. This is fantastic," Savannah told her.

"She's a genius," Clint complimented and kissed Sara's cheek.

Sara blushed. "It's not that difficult."

Cecil laughed. "Yeah, right. Don't let her try to fool you. I'm usually the one that has to try them all and it's a long process."

Sara snorted. "You love it."

The younger man shrugged. "Perks of the job."

"Well, it goes perfectly after the meal," Kurt praised.

"It was a good dinner," Sara agreed. "But I have to say I didn't expect a salad like that from you. I figured you would get one of the pre-made salads from the grocery store."

Kurt beamed. "I know." He looked pleased that she'd mentioned it.

Sara narrowed her eyes. "You did make the salad, right? It doesn't count if someone made it for you." She looked between Kurt and Savannah.

Savannah held up her hands. "It wasn't me, I swear."

Kurt laughed. "I knew you gave me the salad because you didn't think I could make anything else."

"You can't!" Clint exclaimed. "I've lived with you before. I've told Sara the horror stories. Like when you tried to make popcorn on the stove and we had to leave the apartment for two days because of the smell."

Kurt pouted.

The look was foolish on him and Savannah laughed.

"I'm hurt, man," Kurt claimed. He turned his head and winked at her.

"No, you're not!" Clint argued. "So, tell the truth. Who made the salad?"

"I did," Kurt claimed. "I swear."

Savannah leaned into his arm.

"I really did," he told her, trying to get Savannah on his side.

She laughed and patted his hand. "I believe you." He was so adamant that even if he'd cheated, she couldn't have cared less. Plus, this gave her an excuse to invite him over. She could show him a few simple recipes that would impress Clint and Sara.

Sara and Clint didn't look convinced but let it go.

The back door opened and Sheriff Webb walked in from the cold. Sara jumped up and rushed over to help him with his coat. Snow fell from his shoulders and arms.

"Damn, it's really coming down out there," Jim Webb grumbled.

"Let me get you some coffee to warm you up," Cecil offered and rose.

"Appreciate it." He smiled. "Sorry I took so long."

Clint stood also. "No problem. Take a seat and we'll get you a plate warmed up."

"Everything okay?" Savannah asked her boss as he joined them. She wasn't on call for the day, but she would help if he needed her.

The sheriff nodded before accepting the hot, steaming cup Cecil brought him.

"There was a car on the side of the road over off Route 15. Mrs. Thompson was heading to her son's and slid into it. She's fine, but we couldn't find the driver of the other car. The snow was piled on top so it had been there a while," he told them.

"Probably got picked up in this weather. I can't see anyone walking with the snow coming down," Kurt added.

"That's what I figure. The plates are out of state, so it's probably someone coming to visit family. Not used to the snow." Sheriff Webb took a long drink of his coffee. "This is good, Sara."

Sara brought her dad a plate. "Thanks. What state was the license plate from?"

"Colorado."

Kurt and Tony stiffened next to Savannah. She glanced over at Kurt.

"It wasn't a red Mustang, was it?" Tony asked quietly.

"Yeah, it was. Do you know who it belongs to?"

Tony glanced at Kurt. "Colt."

"Oh no!" Savannah whispered. That was not good news. Tony had started to perk back up by the end of the meal, but the worry was still obvious.

"Wait!" Sheriff Webb demanded. "Are you talking about your Colt? The one out with the Church?"

Tony and Kurt stood. Clint was still standing by the table, patting his pockets. "I'll drive."

"Now, wait just one second!" Sheriff Webb ordered, although he rose as well. "What is going on?"

"Colt didn't check in last night as planned," Tony told him. "I haven't been able to contact him and he missed his check in time."

"Shit!" Sheriff Webb looked down at his untouched plate. "Better wrap the food back up, honey."

"Sure, Dad," Sara agreed.

"I'll take Tony with me. Clint, you and Kurt follow us," Sheriff Webb commanded.

"Right," Clint said.

"What can I do?" Savannah asked. She was a deputy and had trained for this sort of situation.

"Ryan and Savannah, I want you to stay here with Sara and Cecil. I don't want to leave them alone until we know what's going on," Sheriff Webb told them.

Savannah opened her mouth to argue, but Kurt grasped her hand and squeezed.

"Yes, sir," Ryan answered.

"Sure," she said, although she didn't like being left behind. She carried a gun and had the authority that neither Kurt nor Clint did. And Tony wasn't even a guard. He was more of a social shifter.

"We'll meet back here. No one leave until I give you the all-clear," Sheriff Webb said before grabbing his coat once again.

The sheriff and Tony left by the back door. Kurt leaned over and kissed Savannah quickly. "I know you want to come with us, but I really need you to stay here. Keep a watch out and be careful. Getting a hold of either one of them would be a win in the Church's book."

She knew Sara and Cecil had been targeted before but hadn't considered how severe the threat still was. It was better that she stayed behind to make sure this wasn't a trick for the church to try again. "You got it," Savannah stated.

Clint was speaking to Sara next to the island. She nodded and hugged him tight. "Be careful and find him," Sara said softly.

Kurt and Clint left. Savannah stood with Sara at the door until they had disappeared from sight, Kurt's truck heading down the road. She glanced at Ryan. "Let's check the doors and windows."

Savannah felt dread in the pit of her stomach as she exited the kitchen to check the rest of the house. The day had been going too well. There was no telling where Colt was or what he was going through. All she could do was hope and pray for Colt's safety while making sure nobody in the house got pulled back into danger.

Chapter Three

Kurt pulled up behind Colt's abandoned car. The little red Mustang appeared to have been there for some time and the sight was eerie. He turned toward Clint, who sat in the passenger seat beside him.

"We have to find him," Kurt said quietly. "He's done so much to bring the Church down."

Clint nodded. "I know. I'll have better luck if I shift. Hopefully, I'll be able to track his scent even with the fresh snow."

If anyone could, it would be Clint. He had been the hunter of their unit. While Kurt had led them on the missions, Clint's exceptional scenting had saved their lives numerous times.

Kurt peered through the windshield ahead of them. The sheriff's SUV was next to Colt's car and the sheriff and Tony were shoveling snow off the roof. Beside him, Clint was removing his jacket and pulling his sweater off.

Their gazes met. Kurt saw the same worry in Clint's expression as he knew was in his.

"I'll find him," Clint promised.

Kurt gripped his arm. "Be careful. This could be a trap. To see who comes looking for Colt."

"I'm not about to let myself get captured again. Sara would never let me leave the house."

"Yeah, and I won't be too happy about it, either," Kurt warned. He stepped out of his truck while Clint continued to undress. By the time he had made his way carefully around to the other side, a huge white wolf was pawing at the window. He opened the passenger door and Clint hopped out in his wolf form.

Clint in his shifted form was a massive beast, one of the biggest shifters Kurt had ever had the privilege of seeing. Clint's biggest strength, though, was his tracking ability. He was known as the best hunter from any shifter species. They needed that ability now if they were going to find Colt after all this time. Several inches of snow had fallen since Colt's car had been left. Clint circled the vehicle several times before stopping in front of the driver's door. Once Clint had started his exploration, Sheriff Webb and Tony had stepped back. Kurt joined them at the side of the road. All that was left was to trust Clint to do his job.

Clint pawed at the snow first in front of the door before he buried his head. He sneezed as he lifted up and glanced over at them. He then took off around the car and toward the wooded area. Tony began to follow, but Kurt caught his arm.

"Let him do his thing first. He'll alert us if he finds anything," Kurt told him.

Tony looked like he wanted to argue but ended up just nodding. Tony's brother Cain was also known as a good hunter, so he should be used to how the shifted needed the space to concentrate.

Standing out in the cold, the snow falling steadily, Kurt started to pray. If Colt was still out in the elements, hopefully he had shifted. That would be the only way Colt would survive. As a human, possibly injured, Colt might even be dead. Kurt didn't want to think like that, though. Colt had been too close to town and reaching the Council compound. But if Colt had been able to shift, then he would also have had the opportunity to get back to safety and call Tony. Finding Colt's vehicle abandoned did not bode well for his situation.

It seemed like an hour before Kurt saw Clint running back toward them. In reality, it had been less than ten minutes. Clint reached him and snarled then took off down the road.

Kurt rushed to his truck to follow. "Stay here," he called back to the other two men. It wasn't possible to communicate when in shifted form but Kurt and Clint had been partnered for so long, Kurt could read Clint's cues. He'd found something, but things were not looking good for Colt. Just in case Colt was found but didn't make it, Kurt wanted to check out the situation before Tony arrived.

Clint was traveling at a good pace and Kurt kept his truck following behind. He covered a mile before Clint veered off once again. Kurt pulled over and waited. He had to wait another twenty minutes. Clint reappeared and disappeared in front of the large trees. Kurt watched as his friend seemed to be desperately pawing at the ground before running around again.

He'd lost the scent.

"Damn!" Kurt slammed his hand against the steering wheel.

Kurt gave Clint another fifteen minutes but knew they were as far as they would get. If he didn't call Clint back, his friend would keep at it until he froze to death. Leaving the truck running with the heater blasting, he stepped out and whistled. Clint's ears perked up before he started trotting over. Kurt hurried around to hold the passenger door open so Clint could jump up inside. Kurt slammed the door closed and made his way back around the truck.

He yanked open his door. Clint was already back in human form and was pulling on his jeans. Kurt waited until Clint had dressed and was holding his hands in front of the heater vents.

"What did you find?"

Clint shook his head. "I don't know why Colt pulled over. But I can scent him outside the car and running to the wooded area. There are two other traces that joined him there, but they didn't go back to Colt's car. They came here. Then I lose his scent completely. I can only guess that there was another vehicle. I followed the odor of another vehicle to here."

"We've got to assume that Colt's cover has been blown and he's in danger," Kurt declared.

"Yeah, I agree. He got out of his car and ran but was picked up here. He might not have walked back to the vehicle parked here on his own. I can get very small traces of blood and the scent of others."

"Damn," Kurt cursed before turning the truck around and heading back to Sheriff Webb and Tony.

Clint remained peering around the area as if he'd be able to will Colt to appear. Kurt wished he could.

He slowed as he spotted the Mustang and the sheriff's SUV. The sheriff was inside his vehicle while Tony remained pacing beside Colt's car. Tony was a shifter so he'd be okay a little while outside in the elements, but they needed to get him safe and warm back at the Council compound. There was no telling how Colt's cover had gotten blown, which put Tony in immediate danger.

As far as Kurt was aware, the Church didn't know that Tony was in town.

If anything happened to Tony, the entire shifter world would be turned upside down. Tony standing on the stage with the other shifters being the first to reveal what they were had been history-making.

As Kurt had gotten to know Tony better and better, he couldn't think of a man who'd sacrificed so much for shifter rights. Tony had made the rounds on television arguing and debating against people who'd hated him for what he was. He'd fought while showing the public that shifters were human as well.

Kurt didn't want to deliver the bad news, but Tony had a right to know.

They needed to come up with a plan.

Where was Colt and how could they rescue him?

He pulled up in front of Tony. Sheriff Webb climbed out of his vehicle. Clint followed behind Kurt.

The four of them stood in front of Colt's car.

"Well?" Tony asked. The look on his face showed that he wasn't expecting good news.

"I followed his scent until I lost it. I believe some sort of car picked him up," Clint said.

"Someone driving past?" Tony asked. "Car trouble?"

"No," Clint responded. "He ran from this point into the woods. He was being followed. I don't think he entered the other vehicle of his own free will."

"Fuck," Tony spat. "He was taken."

"We think so," Kurt agreed. He laid his hand on Tony's shoulder.

"What do we do now?" Tony asked. The desperate edge in his tone tore at Kurt's heart.

"We figure out where he is and we go and get him back."

Tony sighed. "It's my fault he's in this position."

"No, son." Sheriff Webb patted Tony's back.

"It's true," Tony insisted. "I was in Colorado meeting with Alphas to see which Packs would come out to the public. Colt was there with his Alpha. Colt is Austin's Beta and while I was in town, the felines attacked several of us, including Austin's girl. Well, they'd meet and he was trying to convince her to become more, which she eventually agreed to. I was shot and Colt wanted to find out who the felines found out about us from."

"Colt made the decision to get involved because it was the right thing to do," Kurt corrected. He didn't know Colt well, but he was certain he was speaking the truth.

"He wanted to impress me," Tony said. He shook his head before wiping at his eyes. "I was attracted to him the moment we met, but I was so used to being in the public eye I ignored how I felt and him. It wasn't until Cain showed up to take me home that I realized what I was missing out on. Cain had Emily and I was letting Colt slip through my fingers."

Which was why Tony had been able to advise Kurt on his situation with Savannah.

"Tony," Clint spoke up. "I've met Colt. Sure, I don't know him as well as you do, but I get the feeling he'd have wanted to take on this assignment, no matter what. That's just the type of guy he is. He wants to protect everyone and, yes, that includes you. So, let's not let him down."

"You're right," Tony agreed. "I need to call Colt's Alpha and my brother. And we need to figure out where they'd take Colt. Hell, we need to figure out who 'they' are."

"And we will," Kurt promised.

"We'll find him," Clint stated firmly.

"I'll call and have one of the guards come pick up Colt's car," Kurt said. "Why don't you and the sheriff head to the compound? We need to update the Alphas and you can make your calls."

Tony ran his fingers over the hood of Colt's Mustang before walking away.

Kurt waited until he and the sheriff had driven off before he turned to Clint. "We need to find him quickly. There is no telling what the Church is doing to him to get whatever information they can."

"If they torture him, he has a lot of intel to give up."

"I know," Kurt said. "I don't think he'd betray Tony or any of us, but we don't know what the Church is really capable of."

Clint shivered. "I don't want to find out."

"If it's as bad as I think it is, Tony is going to blame himself for anything that is happening to Colt," Kurt said.

"We better find him then," Clint declared.

"Before they kill him," Kurt added.

* * * *

Savannah wasn't used to being the one left behind and in waiting mode. Normally, she would be out searching for a missing person or investigating a crime. Being on the other side was difficult.

She watched as Sara and Cecil packed up the leftovers and cleaned the kitchen. They didn't speak, just moved in and out of chores, trying to stay busy. They worked well as a team, probably from getting plenty of experience at the shop.

While Savannah had a million questions running through her mind, Sara and Cecil didn't pause long enough for her to ask them. She wasn't sure bringing up her fears would be a good idea, though. Savannah saw the worst of what people did to one another. As a cop and now deputy, she'd seen some pretty bad things. Sara and Cecil worked in a coffee shop in a small town. Even though Sara's dad was the sheriff, he also tried to protect her from all the bad in the world.

Savannah didn't want to upset either of them further, so she kept quiet.

Ryan had shifted just after Kurt and Clint had left. He'd wanted to patrol around the house in his animal form. Savannah hadn't witnessed a shifter transformation before and had found it astounding. She hoped to see Kurt in his animal form one day. Ryan had declared the area around the house safe. That made Savannah feel a little better, but there was no way she would be able to relax until the men returned.

Ryan added logs to the fire as they sat around the living room. The front door opened and they all jumped to their feet. Clint came in first, looking cold and miserable. Sara went to him and put her arms around his waist. Savannah caught Kurt's eye as he entered and could see they didn't have good news.

"I'll grab you some hot coffee to warm you up," Cecil offered and left the room.

"How are you doing?" Savannah asked Kurt when he reached her side.

"It's not good," he informed her quietly.

Cecil came back into the room, holding two steaming mugs. Clint sat in the large chair and Sara perched beside him on the arm.

Ryan and Cecil sat next to one another on the love seat so Savannah led Kurt over to the couch.

As Clint filled them in, Savannah reached over and grasped Kurt's hand. He glanced at her and smiled. She turned her attention back to Clint. It was obvious that the man was upset.

"Tony is staying at the Council compound and we just have to wait to see what they want us to do," Kurt told them after Clint was finished. "As of right now, we've been told to stand down."

"It's already been half a day since he missed check-in. Shouldn't we at least go up to the Church's property?" Ryan questioned.

Kurt shook his head. "I don't want to wait either, but we have to follow orders."

The mood in the room grew more somber after that.

"I'm going to take Cecil home," Ryan said, standing. "It's an early morning start for him and Sara."

Sara nodded. "Yeah, we're going to open an hour before normal with the weather and for all the early morning shopping specials. Black Friday is a big deal even here."

"Make sure you keep an eye out for any trouble," Kurt said to Ryan.

"I won't leave him alone until I drop him off at the shop in the morning," Ryan replied.

"I'm going to take off too." He set his cup on the table. Savannah rose with him. She didn't have any plans, but Clint and Sara needed some time alone.

Everyone said their goodbyes, accepting containers of food Sara and Cecil had packed up.

Savannah followed Kurt out of the door, hoping for at least a kiss. He was parked behind her and stopped at her vehicle. He turned to her when they'd reached her bumper.

"Do you want...?" He trailed off.

Savannah leaned into him and cupped his face. "Yes." She wanted anything Kurt could give her. It had been a long night waiting to see if he was okay. If she hadn't known before that she was growing to have strong feelings for him, having to sit and wonder had driven the point home.

"My house?" he asked softly.

"I'll follow you there," she assured him.

Kurt pressed their lips together and Savannah melted against him. Even with the cold specks of snow falling lightly around her, she would have happily stayed there forever, letting Kurt kiss her.

Kurt drew away and Savannah's lips continued to tingle. "I'll see you in a few minutes."

Savannah unlocked her door and climbed into the cold interior. She waited until Kurt backed up before starting the engine and following him at a slow pace. They only drove a couple of blocks before Kurt was pulling into the driveway of a nice-looking house. She pulled in next to him and turned off her car. She hadn't been driving long enough for the heater to warm the interior, so she was still shivering when she pushed the door open.

Kurt waited for her at the front of her vehicle and held out his hand as she approached. They walked together toward the front door. She patted her pocket with her free hand, making sure she had her phone in case the sheriff called her in. Luckily, she'd charged the phone earlier that morning while she had been cooking her dishes for the meal.

Kurt unlocked a newly painted door and ushered her inside. The warmth of the house immediately began to sink into her. She sighed as Kurt helped her take off her jacket. He hung it on a hook next to the door before doing the same with his. They pulled off their boots, leaving them under the coats, and Savannah rubbed her hands over her jeans as nerves kicked in.

Her heart pounded and while she knew what she wanted, taking a lover was always awkward at first. She wished she could just grab Kurt, yank him close and lose herself in him.

But romance didn't start that way. She had to control herself until the dance was complete. Some men didn't like women who initiated sex. So, Savannah pushed her cravings aside and glanced over at Kurt.

He smiled. "I can make a fire. Would you like to sit and have something warm?"

She could think of many things that would warm her up. Instead of naming them for him, she nodded. "Sounds good."

He led her into a large, open and comfortable living room. She took a seat on the soft couch and watched him openly. Kurt bent in front of the stone hearth to start arranging wood logs into the wide fire pit. His jeans stretched nicely across his ass and Savannah had to bite her lip to swallow back a moan.

Her body already ached for him. Hell, who was she kidding? She had been craving Kurt's touch since their first kiss.

Kurt straightened and turned toward her. He ran his eyes slowly over her body. Savannah managed not to squirm under his gaze. The direct stare had her almost desperate to make a move.

"Come here?" It was a question, his voice low and husky.

Savannah rose and stepped closer even as he started forward.

"I want you," he confessed. "I don't want to make a fire. I want to feel you under me. I want to make love to you."

Her stomach clenched and her breathing quickened. They weren't touching...yet. She boldly met his eyes. "Yes."

They came together. Their mouths latched while they used their hands to feel and touch.

"Come to bed with me," he murmured, lifting his lips just an inch from hers.

"Now," she agreed. "Please, now."

His grip was gentle yet firm as he took her hand and pulled her out of the room and through the hallway. They reached the open door of his bedroom and crossed the threshold.

Savannah turned and placed her arms over his shoulders. Kurt gripped the back of her shirt to hold her close. This time the kiss was slow and full of promise. Savannah ran her hands over Kurt's wide shoulders and down his strong back. He lifted her off her feet as he stepped closer to the bed.

She looked up, her gaze caught the large painting in front and she gasped. "Kurt!" she exclaimed. "That is amazing!" It was a picture of wolves standing tall during the setting of the sun. It was just so powerful.

She turned to Kurt, seeing him in a new light. The wolf inside him was a part of him she needed to get to know. Savannah had kept the fact that Kurt was a shifter in the back of her mind, but seeing how much pride he must feel to have the magnificent picture above his bed made her realize that she wasn't just with a man. Kurt was so much more.

His eyes glowed with appreciation. "When I saw that I had to have it. Just felt the connection," he admitted. "The artist is from a small Pack in the panhandle of Texas. When the shifters first came out, some of her paintings were removed from museums in protest."

"How terrible," she murmured. She peered back at the powerful work of art.

"Instead of getting angry or stopping painting, she embraced the hate being thrown at her and continued to create. I was lucky enough to find this one. Her work is some of the most in demand in the art world now."

"I can understand why," Savannah agreed.

"You're the first to see it," Kurt told her. "Other than Clint, because he helped me hang it. But you're the first that I wanted to share it with. It's personal to me, of how a Pack is stronger together than as lone wolves."

Moved by his words, she wiped at her eyes. Not only was the man standing in front of her good-looking, smart and kind, but he had a romantic side as well. Savannah had no idea how she'd gotten so lucky in grabbing his attention. "That's so great," she told him and leaned forward to kiss him along his neck. "I'm glad I'm here to see it."

"Me too." He smiled and pulled her close again. They took their time undressing each other. When they were finally both naked and panting, they climbed on top of the dark comforter that covered the bed.

Savannah lay back as Kurt covered her body with his. His teeth scraped down her neck and she arched with passion. Kurt's calloused hands felt wonderful as he mapped her body. Him learning her weaknesses and exploiting them made her shudder with need. Her moans filled the room. She shook, heart pounding, electricity shooting through her. "Please!" she begged. If she didn't get him inside her soon, she was going to burn up.

"Not yet," he whispered, placing a kiss on the inside of her thigh. "Not yet."

His lips ghosted over her pussy. Savannah spread her legs wider and lifted her hips, asking—no, demanding—that he stop teasing.

The first swipe of his tongue between her plump folds had her breath shuddering out of her chest. She cried out, her body going tight. "Kurt…"

She almost screamed when he buried his head and started to lick, suck and finger her pussy. She bucked her hips and clawed at his shoulders as her body was thrown into ecstasy. Her mouth went dry and she climaxed.

He still had two fingers deep inside her as he moved his body back up. She grabbed at his head and kissed him passionately as he settled between her legs. His hard cock left a trail of pre-cum on her hip as he rubbed against her. She lifted her legs around his waist and cradled him close.

"I can get a condom if you want me to," he whispered.

She didn't. She wanted Kurt to mark her from the inside. "I thought shifters didn't have to use them."

Savannah was sure she'd read that somewhere. She was still panting and barely managed to get the words out.

"I can carry or pass on diseases, but there is still pregnancy to worry about," he told her.

"I have that covered," she admitted. The birth control that Savannah used was a five-year IUD that she didn't need to worry about. She wanted kids one day, but not yet.

"So?"

"Come inside me," she whispered. "Please."

They stared into one another's eyes as he removed his fingers and slowly slid inside. She arched, taking him deeper. Kurt pumped his hips, withdrawing before pushing forward once again.

"Oh God," she managed. He filled her. His long thick cock was perfect.

Kurt closed his eyes as he plunged deep and stilled. It was obvious that he was trying to be gentle.

Savannah didn't want gentle. She hadn't had a lover in a long time, but it felt like she'd waited forever for Kurt. She wrapped her arms around his neck and lifted her mouth to his ear.

"Make me scream," she ordered.

He shuddered.

"I mean it. I want to feel the proof that we've been together."

Kurt moaned then withdrew before thrusting hard.

That was better. "Yes!"

"Yes," he repeated. He opened his eyes and gazed down at her, then started to really move.

Over and over. Retreat and thrust. The rhythm was steady with long, deep strokes.

Savannah could get lost in those clear eyes. There was no doubt in her mind that he saw her, really saw her. He knew who he was with.

Lifting her hips, she met each and every thrust.

Even though she'd already climaxed once, Savannah felt the tingle from her clit through her entire body.

Kurt could move. Instead of unsteady rapid plunges, he shook the bed frame with his power and the speed at which he took her was impossible to follow. Savannah dropped her head back on the soft pillow and just gave herself to him.

She cried out in passion, spurring him on.

When her orgasm slammed through her Savannah barely managed to hold on to his shoulders. All the thoughts in her mind whited out and she wasn't even sure that she could see.

Kurt rode her through the tidal wave. Sweat had beaded on his forehead. If he was still holding back, she might die from the pleasure.

She wanted to feel him lose control, to push him past all thought. She clamped her inner muscles down and bowed forward. It worked. Kurt swore before his thrusts became erratic and sped up. His hips snapped quickly and he tightened his grip as he rode her faster, harder. She lifted her hips, arched her back and just let the feel of him pounding into her command her body.

Kurt threw his head back and yelled, coming hard.

His warm seed filled her pussy and she sighed when he collapsed on top of her.

Savannah rewrapped her arms around his shoulder to hold his head to her breast. Her heart was pounding so loud that he had to have been able to hear it.

She didn't know how long they lay there before he lifted his head and smiled.

"I didn't hurt you, did I?"

"No," she murmured. In fact, she felt loose and sated.

He shifted his hips and she moaned. Her clit ached from the overwhelming amount of pleasure she'd been given. He pulled out and she wanted to complain, but that would have taken too much effort.

"I need a nap," she told him.

Kurt laughed. "That sounds good." He cupped her face. "You'll stay?"

She blinked up at him. Oh, Savannah wasn't going anywhere. Not till morning at least . "I'm staying."

"Good." He flopped over to the other side of the mattress. "I say we take a nap then warm up some of the food from earlier."

"Damn," Savannah cursed. "I left my Tupperware in the car."

"So did I," Kurt said. He groaned. "Somehow Sara's going to know."

Savannah giggled. That was probably true. "It'll be okay out there. It's probably colder in the car than inside your fridge."

"Good point." He turned to his side and nuzzled her neck. "I'll get up in a minute and go get them. Do you need a drink or anything else?"

Savannah hummed. All she needed was to feel Kurt's arms around her holding her close.

Chapter Four

Kurt woke with his arms wrapped around another body. He knew, remembered, who lay beside him, even before opening his eyes. How could he have not? With all the changes that had been taking place, meeting Savannah seemed almost meant to be. She was a strong female who he believed could handle the pressure of being with a shifter. It was her job to protect others, just like it was his.

Any partner Kurt ended up with had to be strong and independent. Even being able to settle down for the first time in his life didn't mean that Kurt wouldn't be up against some dangerous people. The Church was proof of that. But Savannah could handle herself and that made him proud. He normally didn't think so much about his future, but with Clint finding Sara and Kurt being truly happy, Kurt wanted to find a partner to be there with him for holidays and when he came home at night.

There was still time to get to know Savannah better. Kurt had high hopes that she was looking for the same thing he was. Someone who would complete his life.

He rolled closer to Savannah's back, burying his face into her sweet-smelling hair, the orange and spicy scent that he had now come to recognize as hers. His morning wood brushed against her ass and he groaned.

The night before had been one of the most passionate experiences he'd ever had. Making love with Savannah was amazing. She'd responded beautifully, calling out for more and pushing him to the edge of his control.

He gently pumped his hips, pressing his erection against her before pulling back. Her hand covered his on her stomach.

"Good morning," he said softly against her ear.

"Hmm," she agreed before pushing back against him. "It sure seems like it." Her voice was still sleep-laden, but her body was waking up for him. She moved her hand from his and reached back to grip his thigh.

He slid his hand up to cup her breast. He squeezed softly, drawing a moan from her.

"You feel so good in my arms," he confessed.

She turned over, throwing one leg around his waist. "I like waking up with you," she responded, her eyes warm and happy.

He dipped his head to gently trace his tongue over her bottom lip. She opened for him and their tongues met, stroked and teased. She grasped his cock and squirmed closer. The tip of his shaft brushed over her entrance.

He flexed his hips as Savannah sank down on him. She pushed him onto his back, straddling him, with him buried inside. She rose before rolling her hips and coming back down, at first slow and sensual but gradually picking up speed.

She looked like a goddess, head thrown back, body arched while she rode him.

He reached up to thumb her nipples while lifting his hips. She gasped and shuddered for him. Her breaths were already coming out quick and stuttered.

He pinched her nipples and grinned. Her nails dug into his chest as she rode him faster and harder. Fluid and smooth, she brought them both to earth-shattering orgasm before collapsing on top of him.

Once the roar in his ears had subsided and Kurt was able to breathe, he chuckled. Savannah patted his chest before moving off him.

"I'm pretty sure if I woke up like that every day, it would kill me," he told her.

Savannah squinted. "I can't feel my toes."

That had his chuckles turning to all-out belly laughs. He rolled on top of her, making her grunt, before kissing her thoroughly.

"I might never let you out of bed again!" There was no doubt any longer that what he felt for Savannah was true and could bloom into something lasting. He'd been so unsure if it had just been his loneliness causing his instant attraction, or something more.

Savannah grinned at him but pushed him away. "As much as I would love to spend the rest of my life in your bed, I don't think Sheriff Webb would appreciate it. I do have to go to work today."

"Me, too," he admitted. Alone with Savannah in his bedroom, Kurt could let all his troubles go to the back of his mind. But there were important issues that needed to be addressed. He had to find Colt.

It had been hard enough to leave the compound the previous night, knowing that one of their own was in serious danger.

Even Tony had said that they needed more intel before storming the Church. Kurt and Clint were used to action, so sitting back was hard to handle. He'd had Savannah to take his mind off things last night, but now business needed to be taken care of. He hoped the Council gave the green light to make a move this morning. Kurt didn't want to imagine what was being done to Colt.

"Thinking about your friend?" Savannah asked as she rose. She walked around the end of the bed as he sat on the side of the mattress.

He welcomed her to stand between his legs. "Yeah."

"You'll let me know if there is anything I can do?"

"I will." Kurt smiled at her. "I'm not sure how much the Council will allow your department to be involved."

"So, you tell me what you need," she told him.

Demanding little thing. "Deal," he agreed. He wouldn't go against the Council's orders, but Kurt would use whatever he needed to get Colt back.

"Good." She gave him a gentle kiss. "I'm going to use your shower."

Kurt watched her pad naked across the room toward the bathroom. He licked his lips. *Hmm…shower…*

She glanced over her shoulder in the doorway and must have caught the gleam in his eye. She waved her finger at him. "No way!" she exclaimed.

Kurt dropped his eyes to his once-again hard cock. "Oh, yeah."

* * * *

The compound was quiet when Kurt pushed the front door open. The day after Thanksgiving, most of the Council members would have been spending time with family. With the events that had unfolded the previous day, Kurt knew the Council had been called back. Most should have already arrived.

A few guards walked the halls and he knew that, even though he hadn't seen any, several guards were outside strolling around the perimeter. They were on high alert with Colt missing.

He hadn't been scheduled to come in today either — was, in fact, off shift until Monday — but Colt was top priority. Kurt was worried about Colt. He couldn't get past the fact that Colt hadn't called — had just run. And he had been headed in the direction of the compound.

Kurt walked down the long marble hall to the thick door that opened to the office he'd been given. Large windows with dark curtains were directly across from the door. His desk sat right in front of the windows.

He flicked on the light. His laptop sat on top of his desk where he'd left it Wednesday night. On the wall to the right sat three black four-drawer file cabinets. The cabinets were locked, the information inside for his eyes only.

Across from the cabinets on the far wall was a small coffee bar. He walked over and prepared a pot of coffee. Once the rich aroma filled the air, he strolled over to his desk and turned on his computer. He then hit the button to open the window shades.

Dull sunlight filled the room. It had stopped snowing sometime the night before. The sky was still full of clouds and according to the Weather Channel, there would be more snow by nightfall.

He lifted his head at the knock on his open office door. "Hey, man," he greeted Tony.

"Good morning. I didn't expect to see you so early."

Kurt shrugged and studied Tony, who had dark circles under his deep brown eyes. Tony's hair was ruffled and it looked like he hadn't slept. Kurt waved Tony in. "I just started a fresh pot of coffee."

Tony walked through the doorway, while Kurt headed toward the pot brewing on the side table. He poured two mugs. He passed over a cup of black coffee as Tony sat in one of the chairs in front of Kurt's desk. Kurt skirted around his desk before taking his own seat. He took a sip of his hot coffee and sighed. He needed the caffeine. It looked like Tony did too.

"Did you sleep?" Kurt asked his friend.

"No." Tony shook his head.

There were several minutes of silence, but Kurt had patience. It was up to Tony if he wanted to talk.

"I can't sleep. I can't eat. I knew there was a chance of Colt being discovered but…"

Kurt didn't say anything when Tony trailed off.

"Every time I closed my eyes, I pictured them torturing him or worse," Tony finished.

"We'll find him," Kurt promised. He wouldn't stop until Colt was found. He wasn't about to leave one of his own. It was something that had been instilled deep inside him when he was in the military.

"The Council is calling all the undercover shifters out of the Church. If they know about Colt, there's a good chance they'll suspect some of the others. I spoke to Sheriff Webb this morning and he's going to head over to the Church and ask around about Colt," Tony told him. "We can at least do that much until we get our orders from the Council."

"Good," Kurt agreed. "We've got a little evidence connecting Dan Carter with some high-powered people. We can get more. Before you know it, all this will be over and Colt will never have to get involved again. How's everything else going?"

Tony took a long drink of his coffee. "I called home. Cain is going to come out today. I also reached Austin. He's already on his way."

Cain, Tony's brother, was one of the most fearsome Enforcers of all the Packs, known for his protectiveness of his Pack and family. He was an imposing man and had the skills to back up his appearance.

Austin, Alpha of a Pack in Colorado, was Colt's Alpha. Kurt had met Austin a few weeks ago when the Church of Humanity had first arrived. Austin's pack was one of the two dozen Packs that had decided not to go public, but he still backed the Packs that chose to stay hidden. Austin had explained that until all shifters were safe, the shifters who wanted to remain hidden should have the opportunity. He'd opened his Pack lands to welcome any shifters who chose to move in.

"See." Kurt patted Tony's back. Kurt respected both Cain and Austin and having them come would be very beneficial. "With their help, we'll have Colt back in no time," Kurt assured Tony.

Tony managed a smile. "After this I think I'm going to take Colt on a long vacation."

Kurt laughed. "If anyone deserves a vacation, it's you and Colt."

"I just have to convince him."

"We'll all gang up on him if we have to," Kurt offered. "Hell, I'll help you kidnap him."

"You sure your deputy wouldn't have a problem with that?"

An imagine of Savannah cuffing him to the bed flashed in his mind. "Oh yeah, I don't think that'd be a bad thing."

Tony laughed, which smoothed away the stress lines around his eyes. "I don't even want to know what you just thought about."

Kurt hummed. He hadn't ever played around with bondage, but he could picture several positions that he'd love to put Savannah in. Or have her put him in.

"I take it things are going better for the two of you?"

"Yeah," Kurt admitted. "I owe you, man. I was doubting myself so much that I don't think I would have made a move without your pep talk. Which would have been a tragic mistake. She's so perfect for me. I'm lucky she didn't tell me to fuck off."

"Nah, man," Tony said. "I've seen the way she looks at you. She's just as smitten."

"Smitten?" Kurt teased. That was an old-fashioned word.

"It's what my dad says," Tony revealed. "I like the sound of it."

"I do, too."

"I might take you up on helping me kidnap Colt to whisk him away, though," Tony redirected. "I think Austin won't have a problem with it and Cain is always up for some crazy antics."

"We've got your back," Kurt promised. "But I don't think you're going to have to try too hard to convince Colt to go anywhere with you." Kurt had seen the devotion in Colt's gaze as he followed Tony wherever he went. There was no reason for Tony to worry about Colt's feelings.

"I know that in my heart, but my mind keeps remembering that whatever is happening to him right now is my fault."

Kurt blew out a breath. He didn't know how to convince Tony that none of this was his fault. Colt had volunteered to go undercover with the Church. And Dan Carter was the crazy human hell-bent on killing them all. Instead of arguing with his friend, he stood to walk to his desk. He couldn't just sit around while Savannah was putting herself in danger. One of the guards would be around and it might help if there was someone watching as Savannah and the sheriff went to the Church.

Luckily, the building the Church was currently staying in was surrounded by the woods. The woods around here belonged to the shifters.

"What are you doing?" Tony asked.

Kurt grinned. "Just making sure my girl has some back-up today."

* * * *

Savannah peered through the windshield at the building the Church for Humanity had purchased. She might not have been there during the first troubles with the Church and her friends, but she was here now. They weren't going to get away with anything illegal on her watch. She would give her all to the shifters who had become part of her life.

Her body still hummed in remembrance of making love with Kurt. They'd made plans to meet up again later that night after her shift. She knew that if she wasn't careful, she could become addicted to him, and so she had to make damn sure that Kurt and the other shifters were protected.

"This is it," Sheriff Webb said, putting the SUV in park.

Savannah wasn't impressed. The old building was practically falling apart. If they had been there for several weeks, they hadn't spent any time on working on the outside. "Huh." She squinted to see if that would make a difference. *Isn't this group supposed to be tied to some strong political parties?* There should be money for a decent place in her mind.

"Disappointed?" Sheriff Webb asked.

"No." Savannah caught herself. "No, not at all." She was lying.

Sheriff Webb chuckled. "I know. Not what you expect when hearing the stories about Carter and the Church and what they're all about."

"I expected something bigger, nicer... I don't know — a church!"

"Well, this is just one of the chapters. The way we figure, they settled here just to watch the compound. There aren't a lot of members and they're mostly male," he said. "Single, male members, with a lot of muscle."

"To intimidate," she guessed. That would make the most sense to her. Having a threat to the compound was keeping the shifters on the edge. When Colt had been embedded into the church the shifters at least had a chance of coming out ahead of the church members.

"That's my take on it."

"So, what's the plan today?" she asked.

"We go in and inquire about Colt. We did find his car abandoned. We'll demand to see him, to talk to him."

"For what reason?" she questioned. They didn't want to blow his cover.

"We found his car abandoned," Sheriff Webb repeated. "It would be strange if the local sheriff's department didn't look into it."

"Good point," she said.

"The Council also gave me authority to pull Colt out if he is here. Although none of us think they'd keep him on the premises."

"So, we have no idea where Colt might be?"

"No, but if we can get just one person to talk to us, we'll have a better chance of finding him fast."

Savannah reached for the latch of the door. "Let's go then."

Sheriff Webb met her at the front of the vehicle. "Remember that they might have been watching us, so there is a good chance that they know about you and Kurt."

"What?" Savannah exclaimed. She hadn't thought about that.

"They like to watch the compound and the shifters anytime they go into town. When Clint was taken, they kept referring to Sara. I just wanted to give you a heads-up. Don't trust anyone."

"I won't," she assured him. This wasn't her first day on the job. Savannah knew that the hate these guys were spreading could become dangerous, even deadly.

They walked up the old wooden porch steps. Savannah was surprised that they could hold their combined weight as they creaked loudly.

The door whined as it was opened before they'd even knocked. A young man peered out at them with a scowl on his face. "Yes?"

Sheriff Webb held up his badge. "I'm Sheriff Webb and this is Deputy Conley. We need to speak with Colt Knight, please."

"Colt?"

The young man's expression remained the same, but Savannah caught a flash of something in his eyes. *Worry, maybe?*

"Rudy! Who's at the door?" a loud, booming voice asked.

Rudy stepped back as a dark-haired man came up beside him. "The sheriff. He wants to talk to Colt," Rudy told the other man. Savannah noticed the tension that had invaded Rudy when the stranger joined them. Rudy dropped his gaze and shuffled nervously. He wasn't a shifter, but he was showing all kinds of submission.

"Sheriff." The man held out his hand. "I'm Bruce Carter. I'm sorry, but Colt is no longer staying here with us."

The sheriff shook his hand as Savannah connected the name. *Bruce Carter. Has to be some relation to Dan Carter.* Sheriff Webb didn't even pause or give a hint of recognition.

"Where is he?" Sheriff Webb questioned.

"He left here the night before last. Was returning to his family in Colorado," Bruce Carter replied easily. He dropped his palm over Rudy's shoulder.

"Back to Colorado?" Sheriff Webb repeated.

"Yes, sir."

Bruce Carter smiled and Savannah had the urge to knock the cocky, slimy look from his face. She glanced over at Rudy and saw that his complexion had gone pale. *Interesting.*

"I'd say he left about eight that night. Packed up his stuff and said he was needed at home," Bruce offered. "Rudy here was the last one he spoke with. Weren't you?"

The hand Bruce had clamped down on Rudy's shoulder tightened and Rudy flinched. "Yes, he came by my room and said he'd heard from his father and there was an emergency. They needed him home."

The words were rehearsed. Savannah picked up on that immediately — it was obvious even if they hadn't already known that the words were a lie. But Colt wouldn't have taken off for Colorado. He would have gone to the compound. And he wouldn't have left his vehicle on the side of the road for no reason.

"I need to see the room where he was staying," Sheriff Webb demanded.

Bruce Carter stiffened. "What exactly is this about? I told you he went home."

"Colt Knight's vehicle was found abandoned on the side of the road. If he's not here, like you said, then we will be forced to open a missing person investigation. I need to see his room." Sheriff Webb spoke sternly. "Unless you have something to hide?"

Bruce huffed. "Of course, we don't." He opened the door. "Come along then. We are trying to spend time with our family. It is a holiday. This interruption is not appreciated."

Savannah held in a snort. They didn't give a damn about family or the holiday. They just didn't want them nosing around. She followed as Bruce led the way, Rudy behind him and Sheriff Webb in front of her. She sent a quick glance back at the sheriff and he nodded. Rudy was going to be key to getting answers. That was, if she could get him away from Bruce.

The halls weren't in much better condition than the outside of the building. She could smell mold and dirt. If Colt had the same enhanced senses as the other shifters, she didn't know how he had stood the stench.

They were shown a small, empty room. A bed, dresser and nightstand were the only things inside. It was obvious that nothing of Colt's had been left behind, but she still had to search. Savannah started opening drawers while the sheriff looked under the bed and in the closet. There was not one item remaining.

Sheriff Webb sent her a worried look. He turned back to the two other men. "I need to take your statements and anyone else who spoke to Colt the night before last. Anyone who had contact with him the last few days."

Bruce narrowed his eyes before he sighed. "Fine. Let's just get this over with so we can go back to enjoying our day."

Bruce stomped out but dragged Rudy behind him so Savannah didn't have the chance to say anything. That was okay—Savannah wouldn't give up. A little planning and she'd work out an idea.

They set up in what Bruce called the sanctuary. The sheriff took half the members while Savannah took the others. It didn't take long to see that the church was prepared for them. Everyone had the same story. She heard the words repeated time after time, the answers rehearsed and automatic.

She finished her list and saw Rudy standing at the edge of the crowd. "I would like to ask you a few more questions." She motioned him forward. "Since you were the last to speak with Colt."

He looked over at Bruce Carter, who was frowning at him.

"Now, please," she demanded. If it looked like she was forcing Rudy, maybe Bruce would back off. She wouldn't get any answers with Bruce hovering over them.

Rudy nodded and took a seat in front of her. She asked him the same questions she'd asked the others, not surprised that his answers never changed. The sheriff got a reluctant Bruce to sit with him, giving Savannah the chance she needed. She repeated the questions, but Rudy stubbornly didn't change one answer. That just pissed her off.

"You were friends with Colt," she said softly. She needed to get through to Rudy. He was nervous, edgy, just right to come clean. She could work a suspect with grace and a firm tone and Rudy would eventually give in. She didn't have the time, though. The sheriff could only stall Bruce for so long.

Rudy's head bobbed up and down. "He was my friend."

She reached over and grasped his hand. "Then help me. Colt could be hurt. Don't you want to know he'd okay?"

He looked up at her and she saw in his gaze that he wanted to.

"I do, but—"

"Are you finished, Deputy?" Bruce Carter asked, walking up to them.

Rudy yanked his hand away and stood.

Damn it! She just needed more time.

"We'll leave for now. We may need to ask you more questions." Sheriff Webb joined them.

Bruce Carter sneered. "Please call ahead next time."

Savannah remained silent until they were back in front of his vehicle. "I almost got him to talk."

"I know, but Bruce was keeping a close eye on the two of you, so it might have been worse for Rudy. I'm certain they'll be keeping him close."

"I need to get him away from everyone," Savannah said.

"Between us and the shifters, we'll have someone keep a watch out. If he leaves on his own, we'll pull him over and get him to talk."

"There's no telling how long that will take, though," she complained. Colt wasn't going to be able to last long in the hands of the humans if they were as dangerous as she'd been told.

"It's all we can do," Sheriff Webb told her. "I don't think it will be us that finds him anyway. The shifters will tear this town apart. I'm surprised they haven't started already."

So was she. "I hope he's okay."

"Me, too," Sheriff Webb agreed.

Some movement glimpsed from the corner of her eye had her freezing in place.

"Sheriff," she whispered.

"I see," he responded. "Probably here to watch over us. Don't look in his direction."

Savannah had to force herself to not stare at the wolf peering through the trees at them. She didn't know if it was Kurt, Clint or another shifter, although she was certain it was a shifter and not a natural wolf. The gaze was too direct.

She smiled as she climbed in the passenger side of the vehicle. *Trust Kurt to make sure we have back-up.*

Chapter Five

Kurt's phone rang and he picked it up without taking his eyes away from his monitor. His back and neck were sore from hours of looking at maps. There was only so far the Church could take Colt and only so many places to hide him. "Yes?"

"Sir, this is Wes at the guard station. I have Sheriff Webb and Deputy Conley asking for entrance."

That grabbed his attention. To his knowledge, the sheriff hadn't planned on being at the compound or had a meeting scheduled. But they'd been headed to the Church earlier, so maybe they had some news. "Let them through," he ordered the guard. He stood quickly and headed out of his office to meet them.

The guard he'd sent along had reported back that he hadn't seen anything of concern. He also hadn't been able to find any recent scent of Colt, which was upsetting. He picked up the pace toward the door and Savannah.

Ryan was just opening the front door as Kurt reached the entrance. Sheriff Webb stepped inside and Kurt waited.

There…

Savannah followed the sheriff inside and looked up. Their gazes locked and she smiled. Kurt's heart sped up and he licked his suddenly dry lips. Inside he felt his wolf scratch and claw to be let out. His skin felt tight and his teeth ached, about to lengthen. It wasn't a reaction he was used to. He'd always had absolute control of his animal. This was different. He had to shake his head when he realized Ryan was calling his name.

Ryan grinned at him when Kurt was able to focus. Shit, he needed to get his act together. He walked over to join the group. Kurt made sure to brush against Savannah as soon as he was close enough. That seemed to calm his wolf some. Kurt was going to have to think about the strong reaction his wolf side was having to her. But that could wait until later.

"We just came from the Church," Sheriff Webb told him. "You have someplace we can talk?"

"Yes, sure," he said and turned to Ryan. "Can you find Tony? He was going to make some calls, probably in his office. We'll be in mine."

"Sure thing," Ryan replied and hurried away.

Kurt placed his hand on the small of Savannah's back and steered both her and the sheriff to his office. Warmth filled his palm. Just a small touch and peace settled over him. He ushered them to his empty guest chairs before starting a fresh pot of coffee.

Tony and Ryan came back in just as the coffee was done brewing. Ryan helped him hand out hot cups before they gathered around his desk to hear what the two had learned.

As the sheriff filled them in, Kurt stood beside Savannah's chair, running his fingers over her shoulder. He liked just being able to touch her. No one who was in the room with him would find his need weird. For a shifter, touch was simply a way to connect. It didn't hurt that he was also getting his scent on her. Humans wouldn't be able to tell, but any shifter that she crossed paths with would have no trouble knowing who she belonged to.

He absorbed what they were told and it worried him. Colt had been headed to the compound, but he hadn't shifted, hadn't called. *Why hasn't he called?*

"I had Colt's car towed in. There were no personal items in Colt's vehicle," Sheriff Webb informed them.

"And his room was completely empty," Savannah added.

Tony shuddered and Ryan clasped his shoulder in support.

"Rudy knows something," Savannah said. "He wants to talk. We need to get him away from there. I was close to getting something, I just know it."

Sheriff Webb grunted. "Not going to be easy. It was obvious that Bruce Carter is keeping a close eye on him. Probably knows Rudy is the weak link."

"I'll order a guard watch," Kurt told them. Clint was in charge of the guards and could schedule a routine. "If Rudy does leave alone, we can pick him up."

"That's what I was thinking. We can split duty between your people and my deputies," Sheriff Webb agreed.

"I'll get it set up and send you over our schedule so you can fill in some spaces," Kurt assured him. The phone rang and Kurt excused himself to answer. "Hello?"

"Kurt, sorry to interrupt." Alpha Babcock's strong voice came through the line. "I was hoping to catch the sheriff while he was here."

"Yes, sir," Kurt answered. "He's still here."

"Could you ask Tony to bring him into the conference room?" Alpha Babcock requested.

"Yes, sir."

He hung up the phone and relayed the message to the men. The sheriff stood and Tony took him out of the room. Kurt glanced up at Ryan.

"I'll just go check on the guards," Ryan said, rocking back on his heels. "Give you two some privacy."

Kurt scowled after the other man, but Ryan ignored him. Ryan had been hanging out too much with Clint, obviously picking up Clint's bad habit of teasing Kurt.

The office door clicked shut.

"Alone at last," she said, rising to her feet and wrapping her arms around his neck.

He couldn't have agreed more. Kurt took her lips in a deep, passionate kiss while running his hands down her sides. "Yes, we are," he whispered against her mouth. "Wonder how long we'll have?"

"No idea. We better hurry though," Savannah said, and dropped her hand to rub at his erection.

He groaned. God, he was so hard for her.

She fumbled with his button and he placed his hand over hers. He darted his gaze around his office. There wasn't really a comfortable place to move them. Could he even do this? They were surrounded by shifters. If they did anything, in his office, someone would know.

Savannah laughed. "Kurt! Come on!" She dragged him over to his desk and pushed him into his chair. He blinked in surprise when she dropped to her knees in front of him.

Who was he kidding? Of course they were going to do this. He would never turn down Savannah. Hell, he wanted her just as much as she wanted him. Maybe more, because even the wolf part of him craved the connection with her.

Her eyes sparkled as she reached to unsnap his jeans. He lifted his hips and helped push his pants and boxers down his thighs.

Savannah grasped his cock and stroked him. He dropped his head back. Her hand was warm against his already heated flesh. When she bent and licked at the tip of his cock, he gripped the arms of his chair to keep from grabbing Savannah's head. She teased him, licking the bottom of his cock head before blowing across the slit.

"Jesus," he gasped out.

She hummed as she engulfed him. Kurt bit back a curse. *Holy hell!* It felt so good to be inside her mouth. Warm, wet heat surrounded him. He pumped forward gently before withdrawing slowly. So very slow. It was torture. It was wonderful. He pushed in deep again and she swallowed around him. *Oh, this is going to be embarrassingly fast.*

Savannah kept sucking and taking him as Kurt thrust over and over. Her hand wrapped around the base of his shaft and moved over him each time she lifted her mouth. She ran her tongue under the sensitive skin of his head and that was all he could take.

He moaned out his release as she continued to pump his cock. He was still half hard when she rose and unbuttoned her khaki uniform top.

Kurt dropped his hand and stroked himself back to full hardness as she removed the rest of her clothes. She placed her hands on the back of his chair and climbed onto his lap. He helped position her and she slid down, impaling herself on his hardness. She shuddered and arched in his arms.

They found a quick tempo. Their hands slipped against sweaty skin, their breaths came in huffs, their flesh slapped together. Savannah rode him thoroughly—took from him, used him—and he loved every second of it. When she clamped down and cried out her climax, he let himself go.

He stood, gripped her hips and turned. He was still buried deep inside when he laid her back on the top of his desk. He spread her thighs wider and pulled out before slamming inside. Her breasts swayed with each snap of his hips.

"God! Kurt! Yes!"

He snarled, unable to keep the animal reined in completely. His canines grew and scraped against his lower lip. He wanted to bite, to claim her. Instead he plowed on and took his woman—marked her with his scent, and when he came, marked her with his seed.

Savannah gasped, trying to draw full breaths into her lungs. Kurt was still collapsed on top of her.

Damn... Hell, that had been absolutely thrilling. Never had she experienced such...raw hunger.

And she wanted more.

Kurt lifted his head, his eyes filled with worry. He cupped her chin ever so gently. "I didn't hurt you, did I?"

She smiled. "No," she assured him. She hoped for a day when he didn't ask that and could trust she could handle him. "That was wonderful."

Satisfaction replaced the worry in his gaze. "Good… Good."

She giggled. She couldn't hold it back. Savannah had seen his face when she had first stepped into the compound. The pleasure and need in his gaze had caused her body to tingle with awareness. She'd practically vibrated while the sheriff had filled the men in on what they had found out at the Church.

When they had been left alone, she had thought they could have a quick roll in the hay. But what had taken place—that had been so much more.

"We need to get up," she told him when she got control of herself and stopped laughing.

Kurt grunted as he lifted off her. "Jeez."

"Yeah."

They dressed slowly, stealing kisses every few minutes, sharing little touches. It was nice, this relaxed time while their bodies still hummed from their lovemaking.

Just as they had finished dressing, a knock came at the office door. Kurt grinned when Savannah jumped.

"The sheriff's ready to leave," Ryan told them through the door.

"On our way!" Kurt hollered back. He reached forward and straightened Savannah's collar. "I still want to see you tonight," he said.

Savannah lifted an eyebrow. "Try to keep me away." And she meant that. She wasn't nearly finished with Kurt, might never let him go after what had just happened. She gave Kurt a quick kiss and headed toward the door. She glanced over her shoulder with her hand on the knob. "You might want to take a nap before tonight. You'll need your energy."

Kurt's chuckle followed her through the halls as she made her way to meet the sheriff at the front door, where he stood talking with Tony and Ryan. Ryan winked at her when she joined them. She refused to blush. No way was she going to be embarrassed. She stuffed her hands in her pants pockets. Damn it, she knew her face was red.

Sheriff Webb patted Tony's back and waved her on. They exited the large, beautiful compound and hurried through the cold air to their vehicle.

"Alpha Babcock asked that we handle any contact with the Church. He doesn't want the shifters involved. Openly, anyway."

"Okay."

"Colt's Alpha is headed up here. As soon as he gets here he will come down and file a missing person report. He's listed as Colt's next of kin on all paperwork."

"So, there's no way that his dad called him home?" she asked him.

"No, Colt is estranged from his family. Colt's dad lives overseas, so we know Bruce Carter's statement won't hold up when we push," Sheriff Webb confirmed.

"They messed up."

"Yeah, but unless we find Colt or any evidence, we have nothing to charge them with. We work this unofficially for now."

"No problem."

"I want you to patrol around town. Continue your regular duties checking on residents after the storm. If you happen to ask questions about a car found off the road" — Sheriff Webb shrugged — "you're just trying to help."

"Got it," she told him.

They drove the rest of the way to town in silence, both lost in their own thoughts. By the time they pulled up in front of the old brick structure that served as the sheriff's office, Savannah had come up with her plan. She climbed out of the sheriff's vehicle and waved. He honked and backed out of the parking space.

Savannah pulled out the keys to her department-issued SUV and climbed inside. When she started the engine, a cold blast hit her with the heater fan on high. She quickly switched it off, cursing. Damn, that had sent a chill through her entire body.

But she knew just the place she could warm up and question the residents. Carefully she pulled out and headed down the street. Stores were open and there were even several of the townsfolk out walking, carrying shopping bags.

Black Friday. That was what they called the day after Thanksgiving — the busiest shopping day in the United States. Savannah snorted. She hated to shop — did all she could online. There was absolutely nothing that could get her up and out in the cold to run around with crowds looking for sales.

She pulled into a parking space two stores from the coffee shop since there was no space available any closer. She hurried inside and sighed in relief when the warmth of the shop surrounded her.

People stood around talking. All the tables and stools were full. She wasn't the only one to see the advantage of getting out of the cold by stopping by to pick up a cup.

Savannah got in line and was surprised to see Clint helping behind the counter. She'd never seen him working with Sara before.

Cecil was at the register and calling out the orders to Sara. Sara was behind the espresso machine, furiously making the drinks before handing the finished product to Clint, who put the lids on and called for pick-up. Amused, Savannah watched the three of them. They functioned well together.

Before long it was Savannah's turn. Cecil beamed at her. "Hey, Deputy!"

Sara looked over at her when she heard Cecil's words. Her friend winked but went back to the machine she was handling.

"Hi, Cecil. Busy day," she commented.

"Yeah, it's great. We'll make more money today than two months during the summer. So, what can I get you?"

"A large of whatever blend is the special," she ordered, pulling out her wallet.

Cecil waved her money aside. "On the house. Just give me a minute."

Savannah thanked him and stood off to the side so that the next person in line could order.

While she waited, she watched Sara rub against Clint while passing him a drink. Clint grinned and when he reached for a lid, he brushed back against Sara.

Savannah wanted that. The easy acceptance of a partner. Someone to come home to at the end of a long shift. For the first time in her life, she thought she just might have found that person. Was it possible she was moving too fast? Kurt appeared to want to spend just as much time with her and when the two of them were together the atmosphere was almost explosive.

"Savannah," Clint called.

She stepped over, but when she reached for the cup Clint pulled it back.

"Seen Kurt?" he asked.

"Yes," she responded. "I just left him at the compound."

"The compound, huh?" The look that he gave her was full of knowledge.

She refused to blush. "We were updating him on Colt."

Clint laughed. He leaned forward and his voice was barely a whisper. "You do know that shifters have a good sense of smell. Very good."

Crap, she could feel the heat in her face. "We might have had a few minutes alone," she conceded.

"A few minutes?" Clint shook his head. "If that's all it took, I'm going to have to give my best buddy a few tips."

Sara came up and slapped Clint on the ass. Hard. "And if you don't stop teasing my friend, you won't be putting any kind of scent on me for a week."

Clint thrust her cup at her. "I hope you enjoy your drink and the rest of your day." His professional tone was hilarious.

Sara huffed at him. "Can you take out the trash?"

"Of course, my love." He kissed her cheek before scurrying away.

"Sorry about that," Sara said. "He and Kurt are so used to teasing each other they don't know when to stop sometimes."

Savannah smiled. "I don't really mind. I like how close they are. You know, my family only talk a couple times a year. Being around all of you makes me feel closer to people."

"I know." Sara was nodding. "I've been close to my dad since he raised me as a single parent, but I also wanted siblings or extended family. Clint was able to give that to me. The shifters are just so close and connected."

Relief filled her as Sara spoke. It was nice to have someone she could talk to who understood how she felt.

"I take it everything is good between you and Kurt? We haven't had much time to talk."

"It is," Savannah said. "He's so warm and kind and…hot."

"I'll take your word for it," Sara said. "I'm partial to my shifter."

"I know." Hell, the entire town knew. When Sara fell in love, she didn't hide it from anyone.

"I need help!" Cecil called.

"That's my cue." Savannah stepped back. "I'll let you get to work. Maybe we can get together this week for some girl time."

"Yes!" Sara grinned. "I'll bring the wine."

Savannah turned toward the door and the cold weather. The coffee was helping to warm her up, but it was going to be a cold shift. Of course, she had to move back in winter. The mild summers were the best, but during late fall and winter they could get hit with some heavy storms.

It was a good thing she had a sexy shifter to keep her warm at night.

* * * *

Kurt stopped in front of Clint and Sara's house and waited while Clint climbed into his truck.

"Hey, man," Clint greeted, rubbing his hands together. "Shit, it's cold out there."

Kurt laughed. He'd been in and out of the weather all day. He knew Clint had been helping Sara at the shop all morning. But he had to tease him. "Getting soft on me?"

Clint flipped him off before reaching behind him and pulling on his safety belt. "Soft, my ass."

Kurt shook his head and pulled back onto the street. He'd already filled Clint in on everything that had taken place earlier. Clint had organized the watch on Rudy even while helping Sara at her shop.

"So how was your morning?" Kurt asked.

Clint grunted. "I don't know how they do it. Sara and Cecil—they are amazing and so nice. Taking orders, making coffee and listening to people. If you ask Sara what every person said to her, Sara remembers every word. I couldn't do it every day."

"Yeah, I agree. I could never make it in customer service," Kurt agreed. "So I know you can't. How many people did you growl at?"

"None," Clint said quickly. Too quickly.

Kurt waited.

"Three," Clint admitted. "But they deserved it. They were idiots, asking for some complicated drink that no one has ever heard of before."

"No one? Or just you?" Kurt was certain Sara and Cecil had handled the situation.

"I'm never taking a day off again. That way Sara can't put me to work."

Clint wasn't actually getting a day off, since they were headed to check on Rudy and the men guarding him. But Kurt didn't say anything. He knew Clint didn't really mind helping Sara out. In fact, Clint would do anything for Sara.

That thought turned Kurt's mind to Savannah. He had gone overboard with Savannah in his office earlier, shocking himself with the depth of his need. He was just thankful he hadn't scared her away, or hoped she wasn't regretting it now.

He'd had plenty of time to think about it as the day continued. His wolf had been right at the surface. He wasn't as free with his other form as Clint was—he only shifted once a week or so or when it was needed for work. Earlier was the closest he'd come to actually letting his wolf take over unbidden while still in human form.

Luckily, he'd managed to hold back enough and not actually give Savannah the mating bite that would bind them together.

But he'd wanted to. Oh, he really had.

"Kurt!"

Kurt snapped out of his own thoughts and jerked. "What?" he grumbled.

"Nothing," Clint responded, laughing. "You were mumbling."

Kurt shot Clint a glare.

"Anything you want to tell me?" Clint asked, batting his eyes innocently.

Kurt's lips twitched in amusement. The look did not belong on Clint's face. The man was far from innocent. "No."

"You sure?" Clint pressed. "Nothing about a certain beautiful blonde-haired, blue-eyed deputy you smell like? Or that reeked of you when she came into the shop."

Kurt growled. Of course, Clint could smell Savannah on him. He should have thought about that. Well, he really didn't care. He liked catching whiffs of Savannah's scent. "You better not have teased her."

"Who, me?" Clint asked, all innocence, which meant he had.

"Damn it," Kurt responded. "I should kick your ass."

"I wasn't bad." Clint held his hands up. "Besides, Sara already threatened me about giving Savannah a hard time. But you're not off-limits."

Kurt opened his mouth to reply, but Clint's phone rang and cut him off.

Clint answered on speaker. "What do you have, Josh?"

"The target just left the premises driving a blue Toyota Corolla. He's heading north away from town," Josh reported in.

Kurt pressed on the brake to turn around.

"Thanks, man. Keep a visual. Don't lose him," Clint ordered.

"On it, boss!"

Clint disconnected the call and looked over at Kurt. "Where's the little bastard headed?"

Kurt glanced over at him, curious. "Bastard? Kind of harsh, man."

Clint grunted. "You know who we're talking about, right? Rudy was the little weasel that had eyes for Cecil like he was a piece of meat. A man like that messes with Cecil? I have a problem with that. He's nothing more than a bully."

Kurt remembered the scene Clint was talking about. He'd forgotten, but now that Clint had mentioned it, he did recall it. "I'd forgotten. It's weird, though—the way Sheriff Webb and Savannah described him and the way he acted this morning, like he was afraid or something."

Clint snorted. "Afraid of getting busted, maybe."

"Hmm," Kurt murmured. But Colt had apparently been close to Rudy, as well. Colt had good instincts. Kurt would have to think more on it. He pulled onto one of the back roads that would have him intercepting Rudy's route.

"Should we call the sheriff?" Clint inquired.

"Nah." Kurt shook his head. "Let's see where our friend is headed first. Savannah is patrolling out this way. I'll call her if we need any help."

Five minutes later, they parked off the road and waited. They weren't disappointed. Rudy drove by in the blue vehicle Josh had described.

They pulled onto the road and followed him. Kurt saw the black SUV in his rear-view mirror and knew one of the guards was still back there while another would be in shifted form trailing the car that way.

He stayed far enough away that Rudy wouldn't suspect he was being followed. He racked his brain to figure out where he was headed. This stretch of road wouldn't really take Rudy anywhere close to town or… Then it hit him. "He's running!" Kurt said in shock. "Shit!"

Clint shook his head. "No, no way."

But Kurt knew deep down that was what Rudy was doing. He wasn't heading into town, wasn't running errands or planning on going back. He was taking the most direct route out of there. Savannah had described him as scared. And Rudy was running scared.

"You're right. He's running," Clint grumbled.

"Damn it!" Kurt fumbled for his phone and hit the number for Savannah.

"Hey, stranger," she greeted him warmly.

"Rudy is making a run for it. He's ten miles from town limits," Kurt told her. "If he makes it out of here—"

"Oh, hell no!" Savannah grumbled and he heard the sound of brakes. "He's not going anywhere. Where are you?"

"Behind him."

"What's he driving?"

"Late-model blue Toyota Corolla."

"Stay there," Savannah said and hung up.

Kurt took his eyes off the road and frowned down at the phone in his hand. She'd issued orders then hung up before he had a chance to reply. That was how he normally handled a situation. He was in charge, wasn't he?

"Get used to it," Clint said beside him. "These women don't know how to follow. They like to lead."

Amused, Kurt shook his head. Clint had a point. And Savannah was a strong woman. He might just have to learn to follow her lead in some things. That could be fun after all. It might be nice to let go and let someone else have some control over him.

He needed to stop thinking about it, though, because he was getting hard and Clint would be able to smell his arousal.

Clint's deep chuckle told Kurt that he might be too late in trying to hide his feelings.

Savannah couldn't believe her luck. She was only three miles from the turn-off Rudy would have to make to leave town. She sped into place and waited.

Just as she'd hoped, Rudy flew past her—speeding.

She hit her lights and sirens while pulling out behind him. She could see the moment he recognized the sheriff's vehicle. He slammed his hand on the steering wheel and Savannah was pretty sure he was cursing her good.

Rudy flicked on his blinker and pulled off to the side.

Savannah parked behind him and waited. As soon as she saw Kurt's truck in her rear-view mirror, she opened the driver's side door and stepped out. She walked slowly to Rudy's side of the vehicle.

"Turn the vehicle off," she ordered. She waited until he complied before stepping up beside his window. He had already rolled it down.

"Dep-deputy." Rudy tried to smile but fell short— way short.

"You were speeding, sir," she said formally. "Where were you headed in such a hurry?"

His gaze darted around. "Well… I was…"

Savannah bent closer to him. Maybe he needed a softer touch. For some reason she felt a connection with the young man. "Where are you going, Rudy?"

Her soft voice must have gotten through to him. He blinked up at her with wide eyes.

"Rudy, let me help you," she implored.

"You can't," he whispered. "No one can help me."

Off to the side, she heard two doors close. She glanced over and saw that Kurt and Clint had exited and were heading their way. Rudy must have noticed them too, because he slumped down in his seat and began to tremble.

Rudy grasped the hand she had placed on his car. "Don't let them take me! Please! I warned Colt. I swear. I told him that Bruce suspected him! Don't let them kill me!"

"Hey!" She tried to calm him down. "Hey, no one will hurt you."

"Savannah!" Kurt called.

"Back off, Kurt," she told him.

Clint growled. "The hell we will! He knows where Colt is."

Savannah had a responsibility to her residents. Rudy was one of those she had sworn to protect. But she knew they needed to find Colt sooner, not later. She looked into the face of the terrified young man before looking back at the two shifters. She hoped that Kurt trusted her. She begged him with her eyes.

Kurt nodded, although he did not look happy. He grabbed Clint's arm and pulled him back.

"Kurt!" Clint protested.

"No," Kurt told him in a low tone. "Let her handle this."

Clint cursed, yanked his arm from Kurt's grasp and started to pace.

Savannah sent him a grateful smile before returning her attention to the young man inside the vehicle. "Rudy," she said softly. "Come with me. Let me help you. You have to tell us where Colt is."

Rudy was still looking over his shoulder. "You won't give me to them?"

"No," she promised. "I'll take you to the sheriff. He'll watch over you."

"But," Rudy argued, "his daughter has taken up with one of them!"

So, she probably shouldn't tell him that she was sleeping with Kurt. "The sheriff will protect you. I will protect you," she assured him. "You can trust us. As long as you don't lie or hide anything, nothing will happen to you. But no matter what, you won't be going anywhere with the shifters."

He glanced back again. Then he sighed.

All she could do was pray that he heard the sincerity in her tone. "This is for Colt. Colt wouldn't want you hurt, either. You said you were friends. That you warned him. That's something only a friend would have done."

"Bruce will come looking for me," Rudy warned.

"He can. Don't worry." She nodded toward the other two men. "I think they can handle him."

Rudy sighed. "I really did warn Colt. I told him to run. I thought he got away before you came to the Church this morning. I was so relieved he'd left."

"He didn't leave on his own. If he was your friend you need to help us find him."

"Yes. Okay," Rudy said slowly. "I wasn't going to get away anyhow."

Finally! Savannah felt the relief in her entire body. She nodded toward Kurt.

"Thank you," he mouthed.

She opened Rudy's door and held out her hand to help him exit the vehicle. Rudy stepped out and pressed close to her, eyeing Kurt and Clint.

"It's okay," she assured him. She grasped his shoulder and supported him to the passenger side of her SUV. She didn't miss the way he held his body or the limp that hadn't been there earlier. Someone had hurt Rudy, probably Bruce. She wanted to snarl. *If I was a shifter, I'd hunt Bruce down and give him a taste of how it feels to be weaker.*

Kurt and Clint had backed up to Kurt's truck's front bumper, waiting. Savannah helped Rudy into his seat. "Just stay here. Let me talk to them and we'll go straight to the station."

She waited for his nod before she closed the door firmly.

As she walked behind her vehicle, Kurt stepped up to meet her.

"I'm going to take him to the office. I'll get out of him what he knows. If he has any idea where Colt is, I will find out," she told him.

"We're going to follow," he replied.

She looked over at Rudy's car. "Can you get his car out of here? I don't want Bruce Carter to know we have Rudy. I think Bruce hurt him after we left."

"I can pick up the faint trace of blood. You might want to have someone look at him as well."

"I'll talk to the sheriff about it. Rudy's scared to death."

Clint snorted but she ignored him. She didn't know what Clint's problem was but she didn't have time to find out. Any minute now someone from the Church could drive past.

Kurt nodded. "We'll take care of the car. I have some guards just down the street. I'll meet you at the station."

She reached over and gripped his hand. "Thanks for trusting me with this," she said softly.

Kurt just shrugged. "Doesn't seem like there is much I wouldn't trust you with."

She heard the emotion behind the words and her heart swelled with pride. "Kurt…" she managed.

He shook his head and leaned in to kiss her gently. "We'll follow you." He stepped back and Savannah fisted her hands to keep herself from reaching out for him again.

Just one touch from Kurt both soothed and aroused her. She craved him, wanted to feel him pressing against her. Would she ever get enough? What was going on between the two of them?

Shaking herself back to the present, she pushed her thoughts away and back to the problem at hand. She climbed into the warm interior of her SUV. Rudy was shifting nervously in his seat.

"You're with one of them, too," he accused when she pulled on her seatbelt.

So, Rudy had seen Kurt kiss her. That probably hadn't been the best way for him to find out. She needed his trust.

"Rudy?" she asked instead of answering his question. "Did you know Colt was a shifter?"

She took a chance. She suspected Rudy had known, but if not, she was gambling here.

Rudy blew out a breath. "He never said, but" — Rudy shrugged — "I suspected."

"Why?" she questioned.

"Colt joined the group and I never could figure what he was doing there. He wasn't like the others. He was smart."

"And?" she pressed.

"We became friends," Rudy said quietly. "He became my friend."

"Then you know that not all shifters are bad. Just like not all humans are."

Rudy didn't respond.

"Rudy? Did someone hurt you today?"

He trembled. "It was my fault."

"No," she argued. "I don't think so. Was it Bruce?"

"I shouldn't have talked to you."

Damn, so she's right. "We'll have someone take a look at you when we get to the station."

Rudy looked out of the side window after that. Savannah figured it was best to leave him to his thoughts for now. She doubted Rudy had many friends, so maybe she could be that for him. No one she'd interviewed earlier had seemed like they were connected to the young man. He was a good-looking kid and appeared to have a kind heart. Maybe he'd hit it off with Cecil.

She drove back into town with only the sound of the tires rubbing against the road breaking the silence. She pulled into the parking space reserved for her and stopped.

"What were you doing there? With the Church anyway?" she asked.

She didn't think he would answer until he turned sad eyes at her.

"My dad sent me. He's a deacon for Dan Carter," he explained.

Savannah pressed her lips together, not sure what that meant.

"He wanted Dan Carter to make a man out of me," Rudy finished in a voice barely audible.

There was more. She knew it in her gut. More to the story. More to Rudy himself. Colt had befriended him. There had to be a reason the shifter had trusted Rudy. Clint might have a problem with Rudy but Kurt had trusted her. Savannah was going to have to figure things out fast for all of them.

"Let's go inside and warm up," she told him. "We're going to find Colt."

"I hope so," Rudy whispered. "I really do."

Chapter Six

Kurt stood next to Clint, watching through the one-way mirror as Savannah and Sheriff Webb interviewed Rudy. He had to give credit to the two of them. They had managed to calm Rudy down enough to start to pull the story from him.

Savannah was both sympathetic and detailed. She pressed Rudy for his story. The first task was to find out where Colt might be. They had a good idea now of where to look. Rudy had also provided them with names of three people who had disappeared the same time as Colt. According to the members of the Church, Dan Carter was hiding out in Rolling Hills, Nevada, inside the private residence of a close friend. Rudy believed that was where Colt would be taken. Dan Carter would want see to Colt himself. But Rudy didn't know the address or the friend's name.

Sheriff Webb had called in a deputy to check out the lead. Savannah had glanced up at the mirror. Kurt knew she couldn't see him but had felt that connection when their gazes would have met. She'd sent a smile in his direction then had returned to interviewing Rudy.

Rudy was going over the story for the second time when the door opened behind Kurt. Both he and Clint turned as Tony walked in with Cain, his brother. Cain hadn't been gone long from coming to help after Clint had been taken. Damn, the poor guy was getting his traveling in. And he was mated with a young pup.

Kurt moved forward to first grasp Tony's hand before reaching out to Cain.

"It's good to see you again," Cain greeted. "But we've got to stop meeting like this. These humans are really starting to piss me off."

Kurt welcomed him before motioning to Clint.

"Glad to see you're still healthy," Cain teased.

"Yeah, man. I try to make it a habit to only get kidnapped once a year or so," Clint joked.

Clint and Cain hugged. Everyone turned toward the mirror.

"We're getting some good information," Kurt assured Tony.

Tony looked like he hadn't slept in days. Kurt's heart went out to him. He couldn't imagine what Tony was going through. He looked back at Savannah. If it had been Savannah who had been taken, Kurt would have torn the town apart in search of her. And they were just at the start of their relationship. Tony and Colt had been together for a while. Tony had shown a lot of character, allowing the Council to handle things.

Cain was gripping Tony's shoulder as Rudy continued to talk in the interrogation room. Cain met Kurt's gaze and Kurt inclined his head to convey that they would reunite Tony and Colt. Cain smiled back in what Kurt took as appreciation.

Another twenty minutes had passed when Rudy finished talking. Savannah stood and patted his shoulder. "I'll get us something to drink. Maybe a snack?"

"Thank you, Savannah," Rudy said.

As she made her way out of the room, Kurt headed toward his door. They both stepped into the hallway at the same time. It had been a long two hours she'd been in the conference room with Rudy. They'd had to wait for the doctor to check the young man out before the interview could even start. Rudy had a couple of bruised ribs and some bumps and scrapes, but he would be okay in a few weeks.

The strain of the day showed in Savannah's face and stiff shoulders. Kurt reached for her and she smiled. He pulled her into his arms and held her tight.

"He's scared," she said quietly. "He never wanted to be involved in the Church. His dad sent him in against his will."

"I know," he assured her. "I heard." He felt his own sympathy for Rudy. He'd been pushed around and bullied until he'd become what the Church had wanted him to be. The man who had taunted Cecil inside the shop wasn't the same one as the kid in the interview room. There had to be a reason Rudy had acted that way with Cecil. Rudy deserved a chance to explain, in Kurt's opinion.

"He's just a kid," she said with a sigh. "Just wants his dad to love him."

Kurt gently pulled back and cupped her chin. "We know that isn't always possible. But under all that hate that has been drilled into him, I think he's a good guy. I can see why Colt would have befriended him. Colt would have noticed that Rudy needed someone."

"I think it's more than that," Savannah corrected. "I think Colt protected Rudy. Colt was the one person Rudy could depend on."

"I agree," someone spoke behind them.

Kurt and Savannah pulled away from one another when Tony joined them.

"I think Colt wanted to help him," Tony said. "When this was over. Colt would have had a plan for him."

"That sounds like Colt," Cain agreed.

"Can I?" Tony waved to the door. "Can I speak to him, please?"

Savannah bit her lip and looked at Kurt. When he gave her a slight nod, she blew out a breath.

"I can ask," she replied. "You're not an official and he doesn't have to talk to you if he doesn't want to."

Tony dipped his head in acknowledgment. "I understand. But I think he'll talk to me."

Savannah looked torn. Kurt knew she wanted to help, but she was also dedicated to protecting Rudy.

"I can get the drinks and snacks while you two go in there," Cain offered.

Clint sighed. "I'll help Cain. Even if I'm not so sure of this guy's innocence as the rest of you. Anything to find Colt, though."

Savannah looked at Kurt.

"I'll tell you how we know about Rudy later," Kurt told her. "I don't think we have the whole story though." He said the last to Clint.

Clint huffed before dragging Cain toward the break room they'd been shown earlier.

"Okay," she said to Tony. "Come on. But it's still his choice."

Kurt followed Savannah and Tony into the small room. Rudy looked up at them warily when they walked in.

"Rudy?" Savannah motioned toward Tony. "Can he have just a minute?"

Rudy's eyes were wide, but he nodded. "O-okay."

Savannah pulled Kurt back against the wall. They stood close to one another and watched as Tony sat next to Rudy. Kurt made sure that his arm was touching her. It made him feel better.

"Hi," Tony said and offered his hand. "I'm Tony."

Rudy gasped. "Colt's Tony?"

Tony smiled at him. "Yes."

Rudy placed his hand in Tony's. "He told me about you."

Tony released Rudy's hand but reached over and patted his knee. "I'm glad. I'm happy he had a friend in there with him."

"I told him that I overheard Bruce talking about him. I begged him to leave," Rudy said desperately. "I tried to get him out."

"I know," Tony said, soothing him. "And I appreciate you helping us now."

"I want to help," Rudy implored. "I swear."

"You are helping. Colt would be proud."

Rudy's eyes filled. "He said when all this was over he'd help me. He'd get me out too."

Kurt felt Savannah's hand brush his before she intertwined their fingers together. She'd been right. Rudy had needed someone and Colt had been a light in the darkness that Rudy lived. Although Kurt had the feeling that if Tony didn't step up and respect Colt's wishes they were going to have the human around. A lot. She'd almost turned mother hen or big sister on Rudy.

"We'll still help you," Tony promised.

Rudy's tears fell. "I don't…"

"Rudy." Tony spoke softly. "Why did your dad send you down here?"

Rudy sobbed. "He found me and my friend Matt together. We tried to play it off, but he knew. My dad knew."

"Knew what?"

Rudy covered his face with his hands. "That I'm gay."

"It's okay," Tony assured the younger man. Rudy started to weep and Tony wrapped his arms around him.

Savannah pushed off the wall and pulled Kurt from the room to give them privacy. Clint and Cain were waiting in the hall.

"Poor kid," Clint said as they joined them.

"Yeah," Kurt agreed sadly. He vowed that he would help Tony and Colt take care of Rudy. The kid wouldn't have to go back if he didn't want to. He wasn't even doing it for Savannah. The kid needed a break.

"Tony will help him," Cain added.

Kurt waved toward Cain. "This is Tony's brother Cain. Cain, this is Deputy Savannah Conley," he introduced.

Kurt had a hold of Savannah's left hand so she was able to offer her right in greeting. "It's nice to meet you," Savannah said.

"Thank you, Deputy. It's my pleasure," Cain responded.

Inside, Kurt's wolf complained. He had to hold in a growl that threatened to escape. He didn't like another man touching what was his. Savannah shouldn't be handled by another shifter. He didn't think he'd made a sound, but Cain glanced over at him and released Savannah's hand. He cocked an eyebrow.

Kurt found he was baring his teeth.

"Hey," Cain said with some amusement. "Mated wolf here, remember? I didn't mean anything by it."

Kurt nodded but pulled Savannah closer. He knew that Cain was mated. He didn't know where that response had come from.

Savannah looked up at him with confusion. He didn't know what to say.

"Why don't you two get something to drink for yourselves?" Clint pulled everyone's attention to him. "We'll give Tony and Rudy a few minutes before taking in their soda and chips."

Kurt was grateful. If he could get a few minutes alone with Savannah, he'd be able to calm down. Fighting with his wolf nature was a very new thing for him. "Yeah, good idea." He squeezed Savannah's hand before leading her away. She didn't say a word.

They passed the sheriff's office as they walked toward the break room. Sheriff Webb was barking orders into the phone, demanding information from whomever he was speaking with.

"That man should have been a shifter," Savannah said.

Kurt laughed. He couldn't have agreed more. Sheriff Webb was a force. Kurt had gotten to know the man and respected the hell out of him. He was compassionate and kind, but also one of the best authority figures Kurt had ever met.

"Yeah, I wouldn't want him as a father-in-law, though," Kurt stated. "He threatened to neuter Clint if he hurt Sara." He laughed. It felt good after the long, stressful day.

"I think Sara could handle that herself. I even have the perfect knife I can loan her," Savannah quipped, leading the way into the break room.

Kurt tried to hold back his amusement, watching Savannah as she yanked the fridge door open and passed him a cold can of Coca-Cola. "I hope you're joking."

She winked. "Maybe. Although I can take care of myself as well."

"Oh, I am fully aware of that," Kurt said. He ran his gaze up and down her body. She was still wearing her uniform. "You even come equipped with handcuffs."

Savannah lifted an eyebrow before tugging the cuffs from her belt. "These things?" She allowed them to dangle.

"Yep." His mouth had gone dry.

"Do you have a fetish we should discuss?" she teased. But the way her eyes blazed told him that she might not be against the idea.

"Maybe one I didn't know about," he admitted.

She made a sound halfway between a whimper and moan and he found himself closing the distance. She looked surprised before her features softened and she strode into his arms, setting her drink on the table as she passed it.

He lowered his mouth down on hers and he felt the need to consume. He had to taste Savannah, had to feel the bond that had started. Even though they were in the middle of the break room where anyone could walk in, he didn't give a damn. He gripped her hips and leaned into her. Their tongues met even as she ran her hands over his shoulders and back.

"I need you," he confessed against her ear.

"Yes!" she panted. "Oh, God, yes!"

He lifted her onto the table and moved between her legs. He nipped down her neck, leaving small marks. He wanted to claim. To not have to worry about someone else seeing her thinking she was available.

She arched, pressing her breasts against him. He swiped his tongue at the opening of her shirt. He could rip the garment away and feast. His wolf urged him on.

"Shit!" he cursed and stepped back. "We can't do this here."

Savannah was trying to draw in gulps of air. Her face was flushed and her eyes were filled with passion that matched his own hunger. She ran a shaky hand over her hair. "You're right." She cleared her throat. "Damn, Kurt."

He chuckled. It felt good to know he wasn't the only one tormented by their desire.

"Tonight?" she asked, pushing him back before climbing off the table.

Kurt allowed her enough room to stand. He considered pulling her back into his arms but knew he had better not. His cock was already aching — he was so hard, any more stimulation and he wouldn't be able to stop. All he needed was the sheriff to see him making love to his deputy. Sheriff Webb was an understanding guy but that was pushing things too far. Plus, Kurt wanted to be the only one who saw Savannah in passion ever again.

"You'll come to my house when you get off shift?" he pleaded.

"Yes," she agreed. "As soon as we get Rudy settled in for the night. I don't know what the sheriff is going to do with him and I want to make sure he has somewhere to go."

"Okay." He backed toward the door slowly. She grinned, watching him. He left the break room almost at a run. Clint was waiting, leaning against the far wall with his arms crossed over his chest. Kurt lifted an eyebrow. He knew his best friend would have a smartass comment.

"Just making sure I didn't have to pour a bucket of cold water on the two of you. This is her office," Clint supplied.

Kurt flipped him off and kept walking. He couldn't even get mad as Clint laughed at him. It didn't matter anyway. He'd be alone with Savannah soon enough. He headed back toward the interview room. He'd check in with Tony before he took off for the night. He needed to give the council an update so a plan could be made.

* * * *

Totally exhausted, Savannah stood in front of Kurt's front door waiting for him to answer her knock. Once she had returned to the room where Rudy was, things had moved quickly. The shifters had left to make plans. Sheriff Webb had received a phone call from a contact in Nevada who would check into Dan Carter's location. He'd also ordered Savannah to work with Rudy on any evidence and laws being broken out at the Church that would help them secure warrants. Sheriff Webb wanted the Church shut down.

The sheriff was still at the office working on getting a judge to sign the warrants but had sent Savannah home. He wanted her to rest up for the next day. It didn't matter how drained she was though. Savannah wasn't going to miss a chance at spending time with Kurt. There was just something about him that made her feel safe and secure. Her worry for Rudy, Colt and everyone else in town remained in the back of her mind. Her hope that Kurt could make her forget for at least a few minutes had driven her to his house.

So, she stood on tired feet, the cold night at her back, and waited until Kurt opened the door. He reached for her even as the door swung open. Savannah wrapped her arms around his waist and let him hold her. Kurt smoothed his hand down her hair, relaxing her. His warmth against her took some of the chill from her bones. He moved back without releasing his embrace. The door closed securely behind her and she sighed. It wasn't only passion and hunger she needed tonight. It was this, this comfort and support.

Kurt kissed her forehead, then her left cheek, while murmuring to her. When he pulled back to look down at her face, she offered him a small smile.

"Let's get you comfortable," he urged, removing her coat.

She let him help her with her jacket before he bent and removed her boots. He pushed them against the wall and she noticed the bag next to them.

"Are you going somewhere?" she questioned.

He sandwiched her hands between his. "Come on, I put on a pan of hot chocolate once I knew you were on your way."

He led her into his spacious kitchen. The warmth of the room soaked into her. She moaned in delight from the heat and the smell of the chocolate.

"That's a good sound," he commented, helping her onto a stool at the island. He strolled to the stove and stirred the saucepan on top. "To answer your question, yes, we're heading to Nevada in the morning. Sheriff Webb was able to confirm Dan Carter's location."

"That's great!" she told him. "You actually found him. I can't believe it."

"Yeah, we think anyway — a house deeded to a close family friend of Carter's was located in Rolling Hills. With Rudy's information, we believe that is where Carter is hiding."

"Okay." She started to stand. "I'm sure you have a lot you need to do. I can come back another time."

"No!" Kurt said quickly. She sat back down and Kurt lowered his head. "Don't go."

"I don't want to, but…"

Kurt turned and pulled the pot from the fire. He twisted the knob and turned the burner off then strode toward her. "I might be gone several days. We have a couple of guys coming in and will fly out at first light. I want to spend the night with you before I leave," he told her.

Relief had her shoulders slumping. While she couldn't expect Kurt to put her needs in front of such an important mission it was nice to hear that he wanted to be with her as much as Savannah craved him.

Kurt reached over and cupped her face. "Savannah, do you understand what is going on here?"

She blinked up at him. "What do you mean?" she asked, confused. She knew all about what Kurt had to do. Hadn't she been working her ass off all day to help him?

"Dating a shifter is a bit different from dating a human," he confessed quietly.

Savannah jerked back in shock. Kurt was sending her mixed signals. Again. If he didn't want her here because she was human, then why did he say such sweet things to her? It wasn't as though he could claim shifters didn't date humans. Clint and Sara were proof that they did. "I don't understand."

Kurt let his hands fall back to his sides. "Let me make your drink. Then we need to talk before things go any further."

"Sure," she agreed. But worry had her stomach roiling. Savannah was exhausted and thinking wasn't a high priority at the moment. Having a serious conversation? She wanted to cry. She'd be at a disadvantage for arguing toward a relationship if Kurt tried to brush her off.

Watching Kurt move around the kitchen as he prepared her hot cocoa actually hurt her heart. She didn't want to give this man up. Kurt had already become important to her. It was too soon to say she was in love, but she did have feelings for him. He still had his back to her as he began to talk.

"I think about you all the time," he told her. "I crave your scent, your touch. In my office I wanted to mark you so everyone knew you belonged to me. That's something that comes from my shifter side. Once the wolf has accepted a partner it's hard to hold back our instincts."

Kurt turned to look at her.

"Okay," she said. Even she heard the hesitation in her voice. She still didn't get what he was trying to convey to her.

He huffed before bringing her the steaming mug of chocolate goodness. It smelled heavenly, so she took her time sipping it as she thought about what to say. "I don't know if you're trying to warn me off or say you want me."

Kurt just nodded then rubbed his hands roughly over his face. "I suck at this talking shit. But I need you to never regret getting involved with me."

With one palm still wrapped around her mug, she grabbed his hand to hold on. "Just tell me what it is you think I should know."

"With shifters, the feelings we have are strong and fierce. Because of our animal half, we also fall quickly. If our animal, like my wolf, accepts our choice, things progress quickly. It's not instant love, but it can seem like that to others. Our attraction is just intense."

She grinned. Savannah wasn't hearing anything that would scare her off. "So, you've said that you have strong feelings for me and your wolf accepts me?"

"Yes."

"I think there's only one thing left for you to do."

Kurt frowned. "What's that?"

"Kiss me," she demanded.

It took a moment. First Kurt searched her face, and although she had no idea what he was looking for, he seemed satisfied when he pulled her up and into his arms. Savannah wrapped her arms around his waist to hold him close.

She met his lips with her own.

He tasted like coffee, spice and something that she thought was his own unique flavor. She rubbed her tongue against his and ran her hands over his shoulders while settling into his embrace.

When they had to back away to breathe, she met his gaze. "I don't ever want you to hold back your shifter side," she assured him. "I can handle it. Can handle you. Just give me a chance. Let me show you that I want all of you."

"Sweet Jesus!" he exclaimed before kissing her again quickly then pulling back to look at her. "Like I ever had a chance of denying you. You are so perfect."

Savannah was glad he thought so. She pulled his shirt out of the waist of his jeans so she could get her hands on his warm flesh. Lifting up to her tiptoes, she offered him another kiss. She kneaded his back as he plundered her mouth.

It was right. It felt awesome. This man was everything she had ever wanted in a partner. There was a real future in front of her, if she was brave enough to grab it. It might not have been easy for him to confess his worries to her, but Savannah was glad Kurt had. This way, she had no doubts about his intentions and could allow herself to fall for him.

When her fingers brushed under the back of his pants, he pulled back.

"I wanted to make you hot chocolate, have you relax in a hot shower, romance you, show you how much you mean to me," he told her with a huff of breath. "How good I'll be to you."

"After," she insisted. "After you can take care of me. Right now, I need to feel you."

He lifted her right off her feet. His strength always surprised her. She wrapped her legs around his waist as he carried her out of the kitchen through the hall. She nibbled his neck and nipped his ear, causing him to groan as he passed through the bedroom doorway.

He laid her on top of the bed covers and looked lovingly down at her. "You belong there," he said. "On my bed."

She reached for him. "With you."

"Yes." He caught her hand and kissed the inside of her wrist.

She sat up and grabbed the hem of his shirt. "Prove it," she challenged.

They undressed each other quickly. It wasn't the time to go slow. No, that would have to come later. Her blood felt as if it was on fire as he ran his hands over her body. She was already wet for him and he was hard for her.

They rolled around on the bed, marking each other's skin with lips, tongues and fingers. She laughed when he sucked behind her knee then shivered when he ran his tongue up her thigh. He pushed her legs apart before concentrating on her pussy.

"Oh!" she cried out as he started to lick. She bucked up and grasped the bedspread under her hands.

Kurt didn't hold back. He feasted on her, adding his fingers, bringing her pleasure higher and higher until she almost sobbed with it.

It was too intense. Her entire body tightened, bowed as he brought her to climax with his fingers buried inside and his lips on her clit. She rode out the consuming orgasm, going weak under the assault.

She was still vibrating as he slid his body up and over hers. His cock brushed against her folds. Savannah lifted her legs and wrapped them around his waist.

He grasped her hair and lifted her head. Eyes locked on hers, Kurt entered her slowly. He pushed inside, filling her, connecting in the most primal way.

She shuddered as he withdrew and gasped when he plunged back inside. In long, deep strokes, he claimed her body. Savannah gripped his shoulders as his thrusts rocked them. The tempo of their lovemaking sped up gradually until Kurt drove himself inside hard. His head tipped back with ecstasy apparent in his face.

It was beautiful. Powerful. And she wanted more.

She lifted her hips to meet each and every frenzied thrust. His fingers tightened on her hips and her breath caught at his growl.

"Savannah," he cried. "So good."

"Yes!" she yelled. "Yes, yes, yes."

His mouth came down on her neck and she buried her fingers in his hair. She would wear his mark proudly. If having his scent on her made his wolf happy, then the love bites should be even better. The possessiveness turned her on.

"Mark me. Let everyone see."

Hips snapping, Kurt rumbled as his mouth remained against her soft flesh.

The sound sent tremors through her entire body. Savannah screamed out as the most intense orgasm was torn from her.

Panting and shaking, Savannah held on tight to Kurt as he continued to thrust. She blinked her eyes open so she could watch as his face contorted with passion and need.

She would never get tired of seeing him like this. Kurt giving himself over to her and allowing her to see the control snap away.

He slammed forward harder each time. The headboard of the bed hit the wall. They were going to have to do something about that in the future.

As she trembled beneath him, Kurt finally plunged one last time and paused. He lifted his head and roared out his own release. Hot seed filled her and the feeling of completeness overcome her.

Thank God, the Council brought Kurt to her town. Thank God, Savannah returned home.

* * * *

Kurt stepped out of his bathroom, towel-drying his hair. He padded naked across the room on silent feet.

Savannah was still curled up on her side, face buried in the pillow. His heart felt light, seeing her there in his bed. He was glad he'd managed to talk to her earlier in the evening. He didn't like things out of his control. He'd needed to explain to her that what he felt now would only grow, and grow fast. If she wasn't ready for that, he needed to know so he could back off. Luckily, Savannah was on the same track as he was.

He reached down and ran his index finger over the love marks on her neck. It was juvenile, but he liked seeing them. Shifters would be able to smell his scent, his seed, on her but humans could recognize the hickies. He grinned. Kurt felt like a teenager again, wanting to circle around Savannah and bare his teeth at anyone who even looked at her. But the feelings that Savannah stirred in him were intense. He'd not even felt this way about Becca, his first love. With Becca finding her mate and falling in love with Mike, and now Kurt meeting Savannah, he believed he'd been meant to get to this point in his life.

His watch beeped and he quickly silenced the alarm. Kurt had to go but he hated leaving Savannah. He wanted to crawl back under the covers with her and just spend the day loving every inch of her. He sat on the side of the bed and ran his hand softly over her shoulder. She mumbled something and rolled over onto her stomach. He chuckled as he bent his head to kiss the back of her neck.

"Hmm," she murmured.

"Are you awake, darling?" he asked with amusement.

"No," she replied.

Kurt used his teeth to nip her.

"Hey!" she grumbled. She flopped back onto her back and peered up at him. "Did you shower?"

"Yeah," he answered. "I've got to get ready to go."

She frowned and looked over at the clock on the side of the bed. "Five a.m.?"

He laughed at the disgust in her voice. "We've got to get an early start. Everyone has arrived and we're going to take off at first light."

She sat up. He reached over and tapped a key he'd laid on the nightstand. "Here's the key to lock up. I wanted to give it to you before I left."

She lifted an eyebrow. "Giving me a key?" she asked. "I might not give it back."

"I won't complain about that." He looked around. "It's not much, but I love my house. It feels even better when you're around." Kurt glanced away, embarrassed at his confession. It was a lot to throw at her when he'd already said so much the night before.

"Come here," she ordered. He turned his head back toward her. The grin she gave him was warm and bright. "Be careful and I'll be back here as soon as you get home. Maybe once Colt is found and safe, we can have an entire veg day. Naked, wrapped up in blankets on the couch, watching Netflix and ordering take-out."

Kurt almost groaned. *Heaven. That sounds like heaven.* He bent forward and she kissed him thoroughly. With reluctance, he pulled away. When she tried to drag him on top of her, he laughed.

"As much as I would like to climb back into this warm bed with you, Clint will be here soon to pick me up," he told her.

She pouted. "But you're already naked for me."

He grabbed her, making her squeal, and slammed his mouth down on hers.

Her eyes were wide and her breath was unsteady when he released her. "That's just wrong," she grumbled unhappily.

Kurt shook his head and stood. Any more and he wouldn't be ready when Clint arrived. He could feel her eyes on him as he walked to the closet and dressed. He pulled on black cargo pants and a long-sleeved black shirt. He grabbed his boots and socks before strolling over to the bed.

Savannah had the pillows stacked up behind her. She ran her hands over his back as he pulled on the socks and boots. He approved of the touch—just the connection that he needed. Plus, it would have the added benefit of leaving her scent on him.

He turned and gave her a quick kiss. "I'll call you."

"Be careful," she replied.

"I will, I promise," he said and forced himself to leave her behind.

Chapter Seven

Kurt and Clint met up with Tony, Cain, Austin and another shifter, Gray Mason, at the airfield. The large hangers hid their presence until it was time to go.

It was convenient that the Council had their own private plane the men could use. As it landed, Kurt peered over at Clint, knowing how little he liked flying. Everyone seemed relaxed and ready, though. The five of them boarded the plane and took their seats. Clint was speaking with Gray, and Cain and Tony were huddled together. Kurt used the chance to watch the men.

Gray and Clint were talking about Gray's recent move to a town in New Mexico where the community was filled with several different shifter species. Kurt was shocked to learn that Gray was mated to a bobcat. He didn't think he'd ever met a wolf shifter mated to a completely different species. But the smile and love in Gray's eyes as he spoke about his mate showed that the man was extremely happy with his choice. Kurt was amazed. He listened a little longer, making a plan to talk to Gray about maybe taking Savannah there. He suspected Savannah would enjoy meeting new shifters. He gave his attention to Tony when he cleared his throat.

Cain had pulled out a map and spread it out on the table in front of them. Kurt moved over to see what they were looking at. It was a satellite map of a neighborhood.

"Is this the house?" Kurt asked, pointing at the circled building on the map.

"It's registered to a childhood friend of Dan Carter. It was the only connection we could find in Rolling Hills," Cain said.

"I wish we had someone close to watch it," Tony commented. "But it was quicker to just come out ourselves than try to locate someone. The closest Pack is in Vegas and we would have to request help and wait to see if their Alpha would provide it. There's a lion pride of shifters closer, but the Council doesn't have any contact with them. Calling the feline Prince would have taken too long."

"You'd think there would be an easier way to work with other shifters," Kurt mentioned.

"Yeah," Cain agreed. "Even with the word of the Council, it would still be up to the Alpha. And probably take a couple of days."

Kurt snorted. "There's no telling how asking for help from a feline would go. They might flat-out refuse."

"It pisses me off," Cain stated. "We should all just fucking work together."

Kurt nodded.

Tony laughed at their reactions. "That's politics for you."

Maybe, but Kurt would have to think about that. If there was a way to coordinate better, it would be something he'd definitely need to look into. His position with the Council would help with reaching the Alphas of different Packs. Maybe even other species. He had access to the information of every Pack under the Council in the United States. Tony could help with contacts from other countries. But that was something he could think about once he was back home.

The announcement came through the speaker box that they were cleared for take-off and Kurt braced himself. He hated to fly, just not as much as his best friend. Clint had gone pale. Flying unsettled their wolves. Kurt gripped the arm of his chair tightly and closed his eyes.

When the plane leveled out, Kurt opened his eyes and looked around. It seemed the others were just as uncomfortable as he was.

Gray grinned over at him. "I hate that."

Kurt nodded back. "Yeah."

Gray and Clint moved closer and they went over the plan. "I say we head straight to the house. It will be light out, but we should still be able to get a feel for the area," Cain suggested.

"If they're holding Colt," Gray added, "they probably have some kind of security."

"I agree," Cain said. "There's no real good place to shift. I think we need to stay in human form for now."

"Here are two good exit plans." Kurt pointed to the map.

It took the entire short trip for them to formulate a decent plan. Once they had arrived in Nevada, they deplaned to the waiting SUV. Cain took the driver's seat, while Tony sat beside him, and Kurt, Clint and

Gray climbed in the back. Luckily, the vehicle was spacious enough for the five large men.

Cain tapped the address of the house into the navigation system before heading out. Kurt took in the half-deserted airport. It didn't seem to get a lot of business.

"It'll take half an hour to get to Rolling Hills," Tony told them. "There's a small landing strip there, but we didn't want to take the chance that Dan Carter has someone watching it."

"That's good," Kurt agreed. He liked working with Cain. He seemed to have control of the situation. Kurt had gone into missions with a lot less information and was glad he didn't have to again.

As the scenery passed by, Kurt really couldn't see what anyone would enjoy in this part of the country. It was a desert. Even at the end of November, the early morning heat was uncomfortable.

Kurt much preferred his new home in the mountains of Northern California, where they actually had all four seasons. Even as cold as it was right now, there were good points to winter. He couldn't wait for a break so he could enjoy some time alone with Savannah. Soon it would be the season to decorate the house for Christmas. He hadn't had a home for such a long time — it would be nice to put up lights and a tree. He would rope Clint into helping him with the lights outside and was sure Savannah wouldn't mind trimming the tree with him and sip on some eggnog with the fire roaring.

As a matter of fact, he could start planning that now. They could start a new tradition together. Dinner, decorating and making love in front of the fireplace.

Yeah, that will work.

"I'm going to park a couple of blocks away," Cain said, interrupting his thoughts.

Kurt shook himself back to the present. He needed to get Colt back and take care of the current problems first.

Cain pulled into a large grocery store lot and parked toward the edge of the street.

"Just in case they do have someone watching out for them, I think Gray and I should go first," Cain told them.

"Clint and I are pretty recognizable. Tony, too," Kurt agreed. "Sounds good to me."

"We'll walk over and get a feel for the neighborhood," Cain said, opening his door. "I'll try to get some up-close pictures on my phone camera, too." Cain and Gray slipped out of the car.

Kurt's phone rang and he pulled it out and looked at the caller ID. "Hey," he greeted Savannah.

"Just wanted to give you a heads up. We got the warrants. We'll be taking in Bruce Carter and several other men under arrest," she told him.

"When?" he asked. That could add a complication to their mission.

"In a few hours. We're waiting on backup from the State Police. The sheriff wants to offer again to call in the local authorities out where you are."

"No," Kurt said. "The Council doesn't want the humans to know yet. They want to keep this under wraps for now. Tell him I'll let him know if anything changes."

"I understand." She lowered her voice. "We'll try to put off allowing them to call their lawyers as long as we can. You know what a hassle paperwork is."

That would be great. Without a call, no one could warn Carter ahead of time. He chuckled. "Yeah, that damn paperwork sure is time-consuming."

Kurt knew that Tony and Clint could hear their conversation. Tony was looking even more worried.

"We can't stop anyone not under arrest from using the phone, though. They could tip off Dan Carter," she warned.

"I know," he replied. "We'll work it out. Thanks for calling."

"No problem," she told him. "Kurt, please be careful."

"I will," he promised. "I'll see you soon." He pressed the Off button and sighed. "We don't have much time," he told Clint and Tony.

Tony already had his phone out, typing a message. "I'll text Cain that we need to move up the timeline."

"So, I guess all we can do is wait for now."

"Yeah," Clint grumbled and sat back in his seat. They weren't good at sitting around. Both men were used to being in the thick of things. But they would have to trust Cain and Gray. They had to get in and out without being noticed by the human authorities.

* * * *

Savannah marched with determination up the front steps of the Church, behind Sheriff Webb. It was three hours after she'd warned Kurt that they had gotten the warrants and finally they were ready to move.

Hopefully, Kurt had already taken care of what he'd needed to do. She couldn't think of that now, though. With the help of Rudy, they knew where to look for illegal guns and the stack of cash, and she had a job to do.

They'd make damn sure that this branch of the Church would not hurt anyone else.

Sheriff Webb pounded on the door. Savannah rolled onto the balls of her feet, ready for trouble. A young blond man answered the door. He took one look at the sheriff and his deputies along with the several State Police officers and his eyes widened.

"Open the door, son," Sheriff Webb said in a firm voice. "We have a warrant."

The young man stepped back until his back was against the wall across from the door.

"Savannah," Sheriff Webb barked. "Take two of the officers and get to the office. I want everything secure in there. If you come across Bruce Carter, read him his rights."

"On it." She motioned two officers to go with her and they trooped down the hall. She was hoping that she did run into Bruce. Rudy's stories of how Bruce had been trying to cure him of being gay had disgusted her. Savannah had always thought of herself as a good person, but she was really hoping that Bruce found himself up against someone who wasn't weaker than him. Someone who fought back. Bruce had enjoyed torturing Rudy. The evidence was in the scars, and the acts Bruce had performed. Savannah might not be a physical threat but she'd make him pay in the ways she could, legally.

Several people stuck their heads out of rooms, but Savannah ignored them. Sheriff Webb would assign someone to get them out of the way. They had a warrant for all the electronics on the property and they needed to move fast. They couldn't let Bruce erase any data, and they knew the cash and weapons were located in the locked basement.

She turned down the hall that led to Bruce Carter's office as he stepped out.

Savannah held up her badge. "Bruce Carter, you are under arrest for the purchase and distribution of illegal firearms."

Bruce gasped and his face turned red with fury. "What is this?" he demanded. "Do you know who I am? Who my father is?"

"Yes, sir," she responded as she stepped in front of him. "Please turn around." She wanted him to fight, at least try to run. But he proved himself the coward he was and just stood there.

"This is outrageous!" he screamed. "I'll sue you! All of you! I'll own this town when I'm finished."

Savannah grabbed his shoulder and spun him around. "You can try." She might have used a little too much strength shoving him into the wall. *Oops.*

She read him his rights while she placed him in handcuffs. She resisted the urge to make them too tight. *By the book*, she told herself. Everything had to be by the book. If she screwed up this arrest, Sheriff Webb would be pissed and Rudy wouldn't get his retribution.

Bruce was still yelling, but he was also sobbing. With disgust, she handed him over to one of the State officers.

"Please secure Mr. Carter," she requested formally. "Don't let him talk to anyone and don't leave him alone."

The officer nodded and took Bruce's arm.

Savannah grinned at the other officer. "Let's get started." She led the way onto the office Bruce had just exited. Very neat. Orderly. It would be fun to tear the place apart. "We need to log everything, especially any electronics."

The young officer lifted the camera around his neck and began to photograph every object in the room. That would help after she started to go through things. She itched to get on the computer. Savannah really wanted to see the communication from Dan Carter. The shifters had never had any direct evidence of Carter's involvement in illegal activities, but they'd also never had a computer from a Church member. Plus, Rudy made a great witness for them.

It took way too long before the officer nodded at her that he was finished. She practically leaped toward the desk.

"Where would you like me to start?" the officer asked.

Savannah glanced around. Where would the best place be for him to find something they needed?

"Ma'am," the officer said. "You do realize I'm a shifter, don't you?"

She glanced back at him. "You are?"

He chuckled. "Sorry. I can smell your mate's scent all over you. I thought you might know from our introduction."

Savannah shrugged. "He's not my mate." *Yet*, she added, then had to think back to when she'd met the young officer. The State Police's Commander had stated that the officer had a stake in this investigation. "Oh."

That's useful.

"What's your name again?"

"Joe, ma'am."

"Well, Joe, call me Savannah. Do you have an idea where you should start?" That was where this conversation had been going, right?

He pointed toward a closet. "There. I can smell that the man we just arrested spent a lot of time going to that closet."

"Yes," she said. "Great."

Joe strode over and she watched him move with grace. She really did need to learn more about the shifters. Especially with having Kurt as a partner and maybe one day a mate.

"You can ask," Joe said without looking back.

Savannah laughed. "Am I that obvious?"

"I can smell your curiosity."

That was interesting. She hadn't known that was possible. "Really?"

"Yes," Joe said.

"Huh." Savannah shook that new knowledge off for later. "So what kind of shifter are you?"

Joe stopped with his hand on the knob to the closet. He glanced over his shoulder and grinned. "Alligator."

"You can shift into a freaking alligator?" she almost shouted.

Joe winked. "Yep."

"Holy shit." Savannah was at a loss of words. She looked back at the laptop in front of her.

"Well, would you look at this," Joe said.

Savannah gasped. Inside the closet were several filing cabinets, monitors that showed the cameras around town and a couple of computers. "Jackpot," she murmured.

"I think it is." Joe lifted his camera again.

While he was busy, Savannah ran her fingers over the laptop keypad. The screen woke up, delighting her.

Bruce hadn't had time to lock the computer. They would have been able to get inside eventually, but this sure saved time. Savannah dropped into the chair and brought up the email that had been minimized.

The very first message was from Dan Carter. She double clicked on it.

Package arrived.
Will unwrap and get everything we need before we dispose.
Will send instructions but be ready to exterminate.

Savannah sat back in her chair. Dan Carter might be using some kind of code, but it was obvious by the words that he was sending Bruce instructions. And if the package was Colt, Dan Carter planned to kill him. She was sure of it. She needed to get this information logged and call Kurt. And who was Bruce going to exterminate? Rudy? Someone in town? Kurt or Clint? There were so many questions, but she had Bruce in custody and would get the answers she needed.

Savannah took out her phone and snapped a picture of the email before texting it to Kurt.

That was a breach of procedure but she didn't think that Joe would tell.

Joe was cataloging everything they found in the closet.

"Savannah?"

She jumped in guilt as the sheriff's voice came over her radio. She fumbled for the button on the side. "Yes, sir?"

"We found the weapons."

"Ten-four." Everything that Rudy had told them and more. This was going to not only close down the Church in town, but could be used against all of the others. Dan Carter was going to have a lot of explaining to do.

Savannah rose from the desk then made her way over to where Joe was photographing all the evidence.

"Can you pull open the cabinets one by one?" Joe requested.

"Sure." She started with the first and was shocked by how full it was. As Joe clicked away picture after picture, she thumbed through the files. There were folders on each division of Carter's church, including names. That was going to come in handy.

It wasn't until she yanked open the fourth drawer and saw the pile of money that Savannah laughed. *This is a freaking gold mine.*

She looked at her phone. No response from Kurt yet. He should already have landed in Nevada.

Savannah hadn't realized how hard it would be to not have a connection to Kurt while he was gone. Anything could happen and Savannah had no way of knowing. Sure, if things went real bad, Sara would get a call about Clint, but Savannah couldn't count on anyone contacting her. Clint would if he could, but what if something happened to both the shifters? She'd have to rely on the information Sara got. Damn it, she needed to hear from Kurt soon or she was going to go crazy.

* * * *

Kurt crouched next to Cain from their vantage point across the street in the house where they were certain Colt was being held. Cain had been able to determine that the house directly across from the one that Carter was hiding out in was empty. They'd used that to their advantage and had broken in. The front window faced

Carter's place, so they could see anyone coming and going.

He and Cain were watching the front, while Clint was keeping an eye out behind Carter's place, hidden in the alley between dumpsters. Gray and Tony were at the sides of the house. They had all four corners covered as long as they weren't spotted.

Gray had brought along a bag of goodies for the five men to use. They had headsets so they could talk to one another, along with flak jackets they hopefully wouldn't have to test out.

Cain had been right about the security. Cameras were mounted on all sides of the high fence. But it was a chain-link fence, so they could still see through it to the house.

It was a large structure located on the corner of the street and, since they had to stay out of camera view, it would be a challenge to figure out how to get in. But the position of the house on the street was in their favor. There were no guards—human or canine. That boded well for their mission.

"If we wait for dark to shift, we'll have the advantage," Kurt said to the team. Their wolves would give them the speed and strength they would need. But they really needed to know how many were inside first. Maybe the wait would allow them to spot who might be involved.

"We don't know what's happening to Colt," Tony said. "We need to go now."

Kurt glanced at Cain. Cain was shaking his head.

"If we go in without being prepared, they could kill Colt before we reach him," Cain said.

There were several long minutes of silence before Tony spoke again. "I know. We're just so close. It's like I can almost feel him."

"Stay strong, brother," Cain said before removing his hand from the speaker. He punched the wall. "I hate that this is happening."

It couldn't be easy watching his brother suffer and Kurt felt for Cain. Cain was obviously a man of action, so it wouldn't be easy for him to sit back, either. Not when every instinct screamed for him to protect his brother from pain.

"Unfortunately, you're right, though," Kurt said. "If anyone sees us, it'll be worse for Colt."

"Yeah." Cain dropped down and sat with his back to the window.

Kurt took over watching out of the front window. They'd unlocked the door earlier, so if they needed to get out and across the street quickly, they would be able to.

Cain leaned his head against the glass. "Do you think we're ever going to get ahead of the humans that hate us so much?"

Kurt cut his gaze to Cain. He'd not been prepared for such a tough question from the quiet shifter. "I do," Kurt told him. "I have to. We came out for a reason. Everything that we've been through has to lead us to a better life. Or losing fewer lives."

"We were one of the first packs that asked to come out," Cain said. "From the beginning, Tony was on board. Even when I had my reservations, Tony was certain this was best for our people. Now look at everything he's been through. People have tried to kill him multiple times, and Colt has been taken."

"But Tony told me he might not have ever met Colt if it hadn't been for everything he'd been through. I think if you ask your brother, that makes this all worth it."

Cain laughed. "Yeah, he would see it like that. I didn't even know my brother liked guys until he met Colt."

"I think it's more about Colt than what sex he is," Kurt pointed out. "I've seen them together. It's pretty obvious they just fit."

"Yeah," Cain agreed. "When he gets Colt back, they're going to have to have to make some big decisions, though. Both of them hold high positions in their Packs."

"That sucks," Kurt commented. It was a good thing that Savannah was happy to be back in town. Kurt couldn't see himself leaving his job for the Council.

"Yeah, Colt's Alpha already lost Gray when Gray found his mate. Losing Colt would put the Pack in a real bind."

Kurt nodded. "If Colt decides to leave, maybe I can talk to the Council about some strong shifters who might like to join a new Pack."

"That's a good idea," Cain said. "It gives them options."

Kurt liked the fact that he could offer advice and assistance to his fellow wolf shifters. He did want to figure out a way to work with all shifter species as well. Maybe Gray could help, since he was mated to a bobcat and lived with a mixture of species. It was something he really wanted to research.

He opened his mouth to ask Cain his opinion when the quiet of the late day was interrupted.

"What the...?" Kurt exclaimed as Cain scrambled back up to the window. None of their men should have been close enough to set off any alarms.

Cain tapped the communicator in his ear. "Report!"

"Who did that?" Tony demanded.

"Wasn't me," Gray responded.

"Not me," Clint also replied.

Kurt glanced at Cain. Had the humans set off their own alarm? Why would they do that?

"Wait, I have movement back here. Holy shit! Get here now!" Clint yelled through the mike.

"Front door!" Kurt hopped up, and he and Cain raced out of the house. The adrenaline coursed through his body as he ran. He brought his wolf to the surface just in case he needed to shift quickly. It was still light outside so it wouldn't be smart of him to reveal his other form, but he'd do what he needed to protect his people.

"Hey!" Clint yelled. He hadn't turned off his communicator. Kurt put on a burst of speed to get to his friend. He heard more shouts and some arguing.

They raced around the house to meet up with Clint and almost ran into Tony coming from the other direction. Down the alley, he saw five men sprinting toward him. Gray was even farther behind, coming from the side of the house into the alley.

"Go! Go, go, go!" Clint hollered, waving wildly at them. "Back to the car!"

"Is that Colt?" Kurt squinted in the bright sunlight.

Cain grabbed his shoulder. "Back to the vehicle. Everyone split up!" he ordered through the communicator. "The alarms would have alerted everyone to our presence."

Kurt turned and took off. Cain and Tony left in opposite directions.

Colt had been running, without assistance, on his own two feet. That was good news. Kurt didn't know who else was with him, but obviously they all had the same goal. To get away.

Kurt darted down an alley that would take him close to their vehicle. He glanced over his shoulder but didn't see anyone following. He still kept up his steady pace, unsure what exactly was going on. Who were those other men? Why had Clint seemed so excited? He hated not having all the information on a mission. He could adapt. Hell, the military had taught him that, but intel was key when going up against an enemy.

When he reached the rented SUV, Cain, Tony and Gray were just arriving. Cain jumped in the driver's side and started the vehicle.

"Where are they? Where is Clint?" Kurt demanded.

"That was Colt," Tony said. "Did you see him? He was okay. God, he was okay."

"Get in," Cain ordered and they complied. Cain was right. They would have to make a fast getaway.

Kurt strained to catch a glimpse of Clint. There was still no one around. When his cell phone rang, it startled him enough that he jerked.

"It's Clint," he told the others. "Where are you?" he asked as he answered.

"Headed out," Clint answered. "Everything is fine. Head south, out of town, turn west at Junction 520 — it's about forty-two miles from here. We'll be there waiting."

"We who?" Kurt insisted. Cain already had the vehicle moving.

Clint laughed. "Oh, you're gonna love this. See you soon."

Kurt cursed and slammed his hand down when Clint hung up on him. "I'll kill him," he promised. "I don't care if Sara comes after me. I'm going to beat his ass down."

Gray laughed next to him. "I'll hold him down."

"What is going on?" Cain asked with a growl.

"I don't know, but it can't be too bad if they rescued Colt, right?" Tony appeared to be filled with both hope and nervousness.

"But who were they?" Kurt demanded. His best friend was with an unknown group and Kurt didn't know where they were going. "Get your phone out and see if you can find where Clint wants us to meet him."

"Good idea!" Gray dug in his pocket for his cell.

Kurt wasn't going to wait and follow anyone. He'd figure this shit out and be prepared when they finally caught up with Clint. Then he was kicking his best friend's ass. He was serious about that part of the plan.

"I think I've found it," Gray said. He handed the phone to Kurt.

"They're leading us to the middle of nowhere," Kurt commented.

"Away from Dan Carter and anyone who might work for him," Cain commented.

"They have Clint and Colt so it doesn't matter who these guys are," Tony said. "We're going to get to them."

Chapter Eight

Kurt slammed the door closed and stalked toward Clint once Cain had stopped their vehicle next to a dark blue SUV.

Clint laughed and danced out of the way. "Man! You should have seen your faces when you came around the house and saw us."

Kurt growled and lunged for his best friend. This was not a fucking joke. Clint could have been in real trouble and Kurt hadn't been able to do anything.

"Hey!" Clint held his hands up in surrender. "It was funny!"

Tony brushed past Kurt and into Colt's arms. Colt looked a little beat up but better than Kurt had expected. After being held for several days, he was probably suffering. The whole situation was weird. Kurt grabbed Clint. Clint threw his arm around Kurt's shoulder in return. Kurt's wolf settled a little with his partner being safe.

"Let me introduce you to my new friends," Clint told him and waved at two of the men who'd exited with Colt.

"Friends?" Kurt snapped. Clint grinned in return. Kurt rolled his eyes. Leave it to Clint to throw out all the plans and wing it.

"Guys, meet the rescue team," Clint introduced. "Cody Johnson and Zak Lewis."

Kurt shook hands with the two men. Shifters, obviously. They had the animal scent. But they weren't wolves. Gray and Cain came over and Gray sniffed. Kurt was glad it was Gray and not him who had to figure it out.

"Tiger?" Gray questioned.

The large blond, Zak, nodded. "You're a wolf, but I smell…bobcat."

Gray grinned. "My mate."

Zak's mouth dropped open. He glanced between Gray and the others, as if to see whether Gray was messing with him. He cleared his throat. "Oh."

Gray laughed and slapped his back. "I know, man. I get that reaction a lot."

"Wait!" Zak snapped his fingers. "You're the wolf mated to a bobcat in Coyote Bluff? That makes you part of the royal family!"

Gray flushed. "Well…" he said, shuffling his feet. "Yeah."

"Royal family?" Kurt asked, shocked. *How did I miss that? Surely, I'd remember that.* The way that Gray dropped his shoulders like he wanted to hide was funny. Kurt could understand. He wouldn't want to be part of some huge royal family. No, all he wanted was the few people he cared about and his job.

"It's no big deal," Gray said, waving it off.

Cain laughed. "Gray's mate is the sister of the Feline Prince's mate."

"Wow!" Kurt managed. He didn't know what else to say.

Gray's embarrassment was obvious, though, so Kurt didn't press the issue. He turned to Cody.

Cody smiled wide. "Falcon."

Kurt was impressed. He'd never met a flying shifter before. "Wow, again."

"But what are you doing here?" Cain interjected. He crossed his arms over his chest. Yep, Cain was suspicious. Kurt knew that look.

Zak nodded toward the back of the SUV where another man was slumped in the seat. "Our buddy, Jamie. He was being held in the same room as your friend. We figured, as we were saving Jamie, we'd take the wolf with us. Colt did claim that his own rescue team would be on the way but didn't feel like sticking around. So, we liberated him as well."

Colt and Tony joined the circle. "I can't thank you guys enough," Colt told them. He still had an arm wrapped tightly around Tony's waist. "I don't know how much longer they would have kept us. Dan Carter was not happy having shifters around him. He really does believe we're evil."

Tony brushed his hand over Colt's bruised cheek. "It was too long as it was."

Colt nodded and captured Tony's wrist. "I know. But Jamie had been there two days longer than me." He nodded toward the figure in the vehicle. "He took a pretty brutal beating."

Zak growled. "I want to go back there and make every single one of those responsible suffer."

Kurt agreed.

Cody patted Zak's shoulder. "They'll get what's coming to them. We'll make sure of it."

"The fire should keep them busy too," Zak said with a smile.

"Fire?" Kurt asked.

Cody inclined his head. "I've always enjoyed a good bonfire. We decided to leave behind something that would keep them busy as we made our getaway."

Everyone laughed at that.

"We need to get Jamie to a safe place to heal," Zak said, growing serious. "He can't shift out here."

"Do you have somewhere to go?" Tony turned to him.

"Not really. We're based in Arizona. We want to put some distance between us and that house, but he needs help before we drive home," Zak replied.

"We have a plane. Come back with us. We can get the entire story and we have a Pack doctor who can look at your friend. Plus, the sheriff there served a warrant on one of Carter's churches today, so we might have something on this guy finally. You've helped us — let us return the favor."

Zak and Cody exchanged a quick glance. Cody nodded his agreement.

"Sounds good." Zak motioned back to the vehicles. "We should get going, then."

Everyone separated and climbed into the two vehicles. Kurt and Clint moved to the new shifters' vehicle so Tony and Colt could have the back seat of their SUV. Kurt climbed into the back and looked over at the man who had his head tipped back with his eyes closed.

The big dark-haired man peered at him through swollen eyes. Colt was right. The man had been badly beaten.

"You okay?" Kurt asked him.

"Yeah, I'll be all right. I just need to shift and rest. I couldn't take the chance of shifting and giving those fuckers a chance at me when I was vulnerable during the transformation. They would have probably loved to get me in between the change. They taunted me enough about it. Luckily I was able to warn Colt not to shift." His voice rumbled deep through Kurt. The man had to be at least six foot three. He was heavily muscled and broad-shouldered. If the humans had done that much damage to him, they could have killed Colt easily. It was a good thing that Zak and Cody had gotten Colt out for them.

"Kurt Moore," Kurt told him. "I guess you've met this clown." He pointed at Clint.

Clint stretched his legs out as much as he could in the crowded back seat and snorted.

"We almost ran him over when we made a break for it," the man replied. "Jamie Ward."

"Nice to meet you," Kurt said sincerely.

Cain pulled out from next to them and Zak followed.

"Tony should have the plane ready once we arrive at the airport," Kurt told the men. "We'll be able to get off the ground pretty quick."

"California, right?" Cody questioned.

"Lovington, in Northern California," Kurt supplied. "Our Council is located there."

"I've heard about them," Zak said. "Our Prince worked with them when my Streak went public."

"Streak?" Clint asked.

"A Streak is like your Pack. A group or family of tigers," Zak answered.

"Huh, a Streak," Clint huffed. "I didn't know that."

Kurt hadn't either.

Zak gestured toward Cody. "A group of Falcons is a Cast."

Cody chuckled. "He loves telling people that."

"That's not the best one, though," Zak commented. Kurt glanced between the two men. Zak was almost shaking with laughter.

Cody sighed. "Jamie is a black bear."

"Don't go there, man," Jamie warned, but there wasn't really any threat.

"A group of bears is called a Sloth," Cody finished.

Kurt tried to hold in his amusement as Clint laughed loudly. It was hard to tell who thought that was funnier, Clint or Zak.

Jamie grunted next to him. "Every time," the bear shifter complained.

It took several minutes for everyone to calm down. Jamie didn't move, but he did grumble about making kitty soup or something like that.

Zak waved one hand as he settled. "Anyway," he said, "Prince Zachary has always spoken good things about your Council. We appreciate your offer to let Jamie heal there."

It made Kurt proud that the Feline Prince had respect for his Council. It would make things easier for the proposal he was figuring out in his head. An alliance with other shifter species was needed in cases like this.

"How'd you get Jamie and Colt out?" Kurt asked.

"We were following Jamie's trail, so maybe he should start," Cody told him.

Jamie groaned as he shifted in his seat but sat up straighter.

"We all work for the Phoenix PD. I work in missing persons. I had a young woman who was reported missing by her employer," Jamie provided. "It turns out she'd met a man who was a member of the Church for Humanity." Jamie shook his head. "I couldn't believe it. Once I tracked her down, I questioned her in the Church, made sure she was there of her own choice. She was. But there was all this propaganda about shifters on the walls."

"He told us about it, but we just thought they were some harmless humans," Zak added. "It wasn't until we started to really dig deep after Jamie disappeared that we found out they were so well organized."

"And funded," Cody muttered.

"Yeah," Jamie said. "They must have figured out I was a shifter somehow. I was coming home off shift one night and bam, I got struck on the head and woke up in that room."

"Jamie had already started researching the Church and had dug out information on the main guy, Dan Carter," Zak continued the story. "We tracked him to that house."

"I was able to fly above the house to recon it," Cody told them. "I didn't know anyone was with Jamie. I could just tell there were two scents in the room. I was able to disconnect one of the cameras and get Zak in. Then it was just a matter of breaking them out and setting the fire. The fire was so they wouldn't come after us. Although, I'm not really too concerned about it. The alarm should send in the cops and with a tip we left, Dan Carter will have some questions to answer from the local cops."

"That's incredible," Kurt declared with admiration.

"Yeah," Clint agreed. "We were lucky you guys were there. Even if you did get to have all the fun."

"We were glad to help," Zak said sincerely. "Would have been nice to know we had backup if we needed it."

"I've been thinking about that," Kurt said. "I have to talk to my bosses, but we need a way to communicate with the other species. We could have warned you all about Dan Carter before this happened. Then teamed up once we knew where Carter was."

Zak met his gaze in the rear-view mirror. "I'm with you."

Kurt nodded back. He already knew how to present it to the Council. "We can talk more on the plane."

"While you're doing that, I'll call the compound and make sure the Alphas know to expect a few more guests," Clint offered.

"Shit," Zak spat. "They're going to call my Prince. He'll probably show up, especially with Gray involved, and it's going to turn into a whole thing."

Cody chuckled. "You're so going to get another lecture."

"I know." Zak sighed. "He thinks I take too many risks and don't ask for help enough."

"You never ask for help," Jamie grumbled.

"Exactly!" Zak threw his palms up.

"I've got to meet this Prince," Clint said with excitement.

"You probably will," Zak responded.

"We're almost at the airfield," Kurt commented. He pointed to the vehicle Cain drove. Cain had stopped at the gates, where he was talking to the guard. It might be a small airstrip but their plane was there. They would be going home.

The guard waved and Cain drove forward with Cody following close behind. They parked as close to the plane as possible.

"We'll help get you to the plane," Kurt offered.

He opened the door before motioning for Clint to come around to his side. Jamie scooted over but managed to get to the edge of his seat. Kurt pulled on one arm and Clint took the other until they had Jamie up and outside the vehicle.

"I'll get the pilot to open up," Tony called. He was helping Colt up the steps.

"This is pretty nice," Zak commented as he grabbed bags from the trunk.

"Yeah, must be nice." Cody took a couple of the bags from Zak.

"I prefer to stay on the ground," Kurt responded.

"I fucking hate flying," Clint agreed.

Cody laughed. "I love it, man. You should do it without being trapped inside a big metal container."

"Oh." That was about all Kurt could say. He hadn't thought about Cody being able to fly. "Why don't you just meet us in California?"

"I could," Cody replied with a grin. "But I would be pretty damn tired."

"Good point." Kurt shuffled with Jamie and Clint until they got to the steps leading up to the door. Tony had already taken Colt inside. It took some maneuvering and Cain coming out to help, but eventually they had Jamie lying on the couch resting. The rest of the shifters took seats around him.

"The pilot will take off as soon as he gets the go," Tony said. He sat next to Colt with his arm around

Colt's shoulder. Kurt didn't think that Tony would be letting Colt out of his sight for a very long time.

"I'll be glad to get home," Kurt admitted. "The Council finally has the proof we need to take down every chapter of the Church."

"How do you know?" Cain questioned.

Kurt held up his phone. He'd had it off, but as soon as he'd sat down he'd powered the cell back on. Message after message had come through from Savannah. "The warrant the sheriff served today resulted in them collecting every electronic device the Church had. Plus, they found a stash of guns, money and more. Dan Carter and his entire network are going down. Finally."

A round of cheers went up.

"Okay." Kurt waved his hand. "We still have work to do. I plan to talk to the Council about setting up a network or agency of different shifter species. We need help. Each species only working for themselves isn't productive to keeping us safe. The humans have banded together and now it's time for us to do the same."

"I agree," Cody said. "Dan Carter wasn't even on our radar before Jamie's missing person investigation, but according to Colt he's been acting out against shifters for a while now."

"How would that even work, though?" Clint questioned. "Putting different species together?"

"I've been giving that a lot of thought. I wanted to talk to Tony and Gray to get their opinions, but I think we need a shifter-based organization."

"With what purpose?" Tony asked.

"To protect innocent shifters but also as a way to make sure shifters follow laws as well. Right now, humans are fearing us because they know we're faster, stronger and there's not much they can do to stop us."

Tony was nodding. "It's a good idea. Like the FBI for shifters."

"I can see it," Gray said.

"I'll talk to the Council and get their ideas, but I wanted to see if I would have all of your support."

"Whatever you need," Tony told him.

"Absolutely," Gray added.

"I'd like to sit down with you and your Council. I might have some ideas to add to it," Cody said.

"Great." Kurt rubbed his palms together. He sat back in his chair and opened the last message from Savannah. He read it again, knowing he had a huge smile on his face.

Missing you. Hope to see you tonight. It will be cold without you.

He wouldn't let her be cold tonight. After everything got settled, he would find her and make sure she was warm and sated.

"Oh, man!" Clint exclaimed. "He's thinking about Savannah again."

Kurt looked up and everyone was staring at him. "What?" He flushed. Yeah, he'd gotten caught up in his own thoughts.

Clint cackled at him. "I asked if you still wanted me to call the compound. But never mind, I'll do it while you fantasize about your woman."

Kurt flipped his best friend off. "Whatever, man. Like you're not just as bad."

Clint rose then pulled his phone out of his pocket as he made his way toward the back of the plane.

Kurt nodded to where Jamie was resting. "I'll get some water for Jamie. Anyone else need anything?"

"I'm starving," Colt said. "Do we have anything to eat? They didn't feed us at all."

Jamie's stomach growled and he opened his eyes. "Water sounds good, but I wouldn't mind some food, too."

Colt and Jamie being starved was almost too much for Kurt to deal with. Kurt knew that they'd suffered and come close to being killed, but there was just something about letting a man starve that made Kurt sick.

Dan Carter had to pay.

If Kurt did nothing else, he'd see Dan Carter taken down. "Okay, let me see what I can scrounge up." Kurt rose, following behind Clint. As Clint spoke to what sounded like Alpha Babcock, he began to pull out cold sodas. Kurt opened the cabinet above his head and found snacks. Clint winked at him and Kurt chuckled. He could laugh now. Colt was back safe and he had a woman to get home to.

* * * *

Savannah peered through the peephole and saw Kurt standing on her front porch. She yanked the door open. "Kurt."

"Hey," he said with a small smile. He looked so tired.

She reached out and grasped his hands, pulling him inside. The bitter cold night air came in with him. It was past midnight. That meant he'd been awake and working for over twenty hours.

"I didn't think you would make it back so fast," she said, pulling off his coat.

"Me neither," he replied before he turned and cupped her face. "We had to get out of there quick." His hands were chilled, but Savannah didn't complain. Especially not when he dipped his head and pressed his lips to hers. The kiss was brief but enough to show her that there would be more heat later.

"Hi," he said simply.

"Hi," she repeated. Kurt wasn't acting as if anything bad had happened, so she tried to relax.

"I know it's late, but I had a hell of a day and I needed to see you."

She beamed, grateful that he had felt the desire to be with her. "Come tell me about it," she requested, pulling him into the living room.

Her rental unit wasn't as spacious as his house, but the living room was comfy and warm. She pushed him down onto the couch and dropped to her knees to remove his boots and socks. Once she had them off and stowed under the coffee table, she grabbed the blanket from the back of the couch.

She sat close to him and pulled the blanket over both of them. "Are you injured?" she asked, even as she was afraid of the answer.

"No, we didn't even get to rescue Colt. Someone beat us to it."

"What?" she cried. "What!"

He barked out a laugh. "Yeah, two shifters broke in to rescue their friend who was being held with Colt. We were outside still watching the house when they busted out."

"That's…uh…" Savannah's thoughts raced. "Then… What does that mean?"

Kurt shook his head. "We didn't even consider that other shifters were in danger. We were protecting our wolves but leaving everyone else out there on their own. There is no way to communicate between the hundreds of shifter species."

He made a really good point. If Carter was going after the wolf shifters, what would keep him from targeting all shifters? "So, what happens now?"

"I proposed an alliance for all shifters," Kurt informed her. "The Council agreed it was a good idea. Tomorrow morning we'll talk about the logistics and meet with the shifters we brought back with us. They're staying at the compound as Jamie heals. He was the one being held with Colt."

"And Colt and Jamie are okay?"

"Yes, they were beat up some but will be fine."

She rubbed her hands over his. "Good, that's good at least." Kurt was back and that was what she wanted to focus on. Savannah still had a lot of work in front of her to take down Carter once and for all. And things were about to get messy. The sheriff had called in the big guns.

"The shifters seem like pretty good guys. They offered to help with my idea. I think you'll like them," he said as he slid an arm around her shoulder.

"Oh," she replied, pleased. "Will I?" That had to mean that Kurt wanted her to meet them, right? She didn't think he'd keep her hidden away or a secret, but introducing her to the other shifters meant something. It had to.

"Yes, I plan to show you off while they're here," Kurt told her.

"Sounds good." She cuddled into him. "I would be proud to have you show me off."

Kurt laughed at her tone, which was what she'd wanted. He'd had a hard day and it was good to hear his voice lose some of the tension it held.

"What about the investigation into Dan Carter and the other branches of the Church?" he asked.

"The sheriff has called in the FBI." They might have made a big dent in the local branch, but there was still a danger to Kurt and the other shifters from other church divisions.

"I guess that's the best thing." Kurt didn't look happy though.

"Sheriff says it's time to take all the evidence we have to the big dogs."

"We'll have even more now that we have Zak's, Cody's and Jamie's accounts," Kurt told her. "I'll take you and the sheriff to the compound in the morning to talk to them. They're all cops in Arizona."

"Cops?"

"They are detectives with the Phoenix PD."

Savannah scrubbed her hands over her face. "This is going to be a mess. I bet they didn't have permission to enter Nevada to save their friend. The feds are going to be pissed at them and us. We never should have let you go either. The sheriff could lose his job."

"Hey…" Kurt turned her head and forced her to look up at him. "It'll be okay. Just wait and see. The Council will deal with the FBI and all this will work out. Sheriff Webb is Clint's family. We're not going to let anything happen to him. I'll be right here to make certain."

She closed her eyes and rested her forehead against his chest. "I hope you're right," she confessed. "I'm pretty sure I need to see you, to feel you, every day."

"You will," he said, and she heard the promise in his words. She tilted her head back and reached up to bring his lips to meet hers.

She needed him. Had to have him right then. Savannah moved and straddled his hips without taking her mouth from his, gripping the back of his neck to hold him close. It wasn't enough. She rocked up into him, trying to get even closer.

"Hey." Kurt gripped her chin, making her stop. "It's okay."

Savannah breathed deeply. Her hands were shaking. "Kurt…" She needed him so much. Everything was getting complicated and she was tired, just exhausted from all the events from the last several days.

"I know," he soothed her. "I know what you need."

"Please." She would beg for him to take away all the stress and the unknown if that was what he wanted.

He scooted forward, pushing her off his lap to stand. He followed her up. "Let's go to bed."

Savannah took his hand and pulled him through the small house to the bedroom. Once inside, she led him to the bed and urged him to sit. Savannah stood between his legs before she pulled Kurt's shirt over his head. She let the garment fall to the ground before leaning over and kissing up his neck.

His hands came to her hips, but now that he'd slowed her down, she was determined to show Kurt the greatest pleasure he'd ever had. She pressed against his shoulders so he lay back then trailed her fingers down his stomach. She unfastened his pants and pulled them down. He lifted his hips to assist her.

She kneeled over him, kissing and sucking her way from his belly button to his hard cock. She grasped the base and tongued him.

His breath caught and his hips rose. She smiled before lowering her head and opening her mouth to engulf him.

"Yes," he hissed out.

She bobbed her head, licking and sucking, paying close attention to the underside of his cockhead, where she knew he was sensitive.

Kurt bucked up into her mouth. She thrived on hearing the desperate sounds coming out of him. He tasted salty and just a tad bitter—good, a flavor that was all his own.

She stroked with her hand while going down on him, waiting until he was almost begging before popping off him. She released his cock and rubbed her hands up his thighs before she rose and skimmed her body up his.

When she reached his mouth, she took control, thrusting her tongue inside. She positioned herself over him, his cock at her entrance. She sat up and lowered herself down.

He filled her. *Oh, God!* It felt so good to take him inside.

Once he was in her completely, she paused. She looked down at Kurt. His bright eyes glowed up at her. She twined the fingers of both hands with his. Using her knees, she started to rise. Her head fell back at the smooth, arousing sensation. She slammed herself back down.

Yes, she thought. *That's it.*

She rode him slowly, tenderly, rising and falling, with their fingers locked together and moans escaping from her throat. She warmed, heated, sweated. Her body tightened and her clit throbbed.

Almost there. Almost. She released his hands to grip his chest for better leverage. She sped up her pace. Almost out of nowhere, the pleasure swamped her. Her body drew tight and she climaxed. It was huge. Her vision blurred and her head felt as if it was full of cotton.

She came back to herself and Kurt was gripping her hard. She peered down at him.

He smiled back. "You back with me?"

She nodded.

"Good." He rolled them until she was under his body. He withdrew, gaze locked on hers, before plunging deep. She cried out in ecstasy and bowed up.

The time for tenderness was over, apparently.

Kurt thrust in quick, short bursts, demanding that her body come alive again. She scored her nails down his back, making him hiss. His hips moved faster.

"Again," he panted. "Come with me again."

She didn't have a choice. She could already feel the next orgasm building. She grabbed the back of his neck and yanked him down. "Mark me."

He closed his mouth over the soft skin above her collarbone and sucked. Savannah knew how much Kurt liked others knowing she belonged to him. Hell, she thought it was hot as well.

She screamed as pleasure was ripped out of her.

This time her sight actually blacked out for an instant. She vaguely heard him yell before feeling him find his own release.

He collapsed on top of her. She wrapped her arms around his neck and sighed. Making love with Kurt kept getting better and better. If this was what she had to look forward to, she wasn't sure she would be able to survive it.

"I'm so glad I came here tonight." Kurt lifted his head. He peered around before grinning. "Although you could probably hang a picture or two."

Savannah groaned. "I know."

Kurt pulled out of her before flopping down beside her on the mattress.

"Will you stay the night?" she asked. Savannah moved to lie against his side with her head on his chest.

"Of course." He carded his fingers through her hair. "That's why I came here instead of going home or sleeping at the compound. I wanted to go to sleep with you in my arms and wake up next to you."

He said the sweetest things. And Savannah knew that he meant him.

With her cheek resting against his heart, she could hear the steady beating. Savannah closed her eyes. She'd been asleep before Kurt had woken her with a knock on the door, but she was glad that he'd come to her. Not only because the sex was fantastic, but also because she felt safe with Kurt.

"Stop thinking and go to sleep," Kurt murmured.

Savannah grinned. He was looking out for her even though he must be exhausted.

"You go to sleep," she responded.

Kurt's warm chuckle filled the room. Yes, Savannah was going to make sure that she was in Kurt's bed or he was in hers every night.

Chapter Nine

Savannah ran her sweaty palms across the knees of her jeans as Kurt pulled up in front of the compound. She'd been inside before, but this time it was different. Kurt had told her that he'd be claiming her in a relationship with him so the other shifters would know. He wanted her protected if he was unable to do it himself.

While she was pleased that Kurt wanted to tell everyone they were together, she was nervous. What if the Council Kurt worked for or his friends didn't approve? What if they didn't like her?

"Everything is going to be fine." Kurt reached over and grasped her hand. "I would never let anyone hurt you."

"I know," she responded. "I just don't want to let you down."

"Never," he said. Kurt raised her hand to his mouth and kissed the top. "I'm proud to introduce you as someone special."

The doubt didn't leave her, but Savannah settled a little. She peered up at the massive building that housed the most powerful shifters in the country. Now that Savannah was with Kurt, she was learning so much about the shifters and her town. There was a rich past, with how the shifters had decided to settle there and how they protected the humans. An early understanding between the shifters and townsfolk had seen centuries of safety for humans and shifters alike. Savannah understood the bond the wolves had with the town because of the length of time they'd been there.

"Are you ready?" Kurt asked. "The sheriff will be here soon."

Savannah shook her thoughts away. "Sorry."

He smiled at her before he climbed out of the vehicle. Savannah hurried to follow behind him and met Kurt at the front of his truck. He held out his hand and she took it happily. Kurt led her up the steps and the door opened before they reached it.

Clint stepped out as he grinned at them. "Good morning."

Kurt was scowling at him.

"Heya, Clint," Savannah greeted.

Clint nodded at her before he winked at Kurt. "Running late?"

Savannah refused to blush. She'd learned how much Kurt and Clint loved to give each other a hard time. And it was her fault they were late. She'd teased Kurt as they'd eaten breakfast so when she went to shower he'd joined her. That had turned her normal fifteen-minute shower into a long, forty-minute, pleasure-filled event. They'd been late after that.

"Shut up, Clint, or I'll tell Sara about that time you went down to Mexico, where you met that—"

"Okay!" Clint held up his hands. "That's wrong, man. You're supposed to keep my secrets."

Savannah laughed. Clint could act like the biggest teenager, but he was also a good guy.

"Move out of the way." Kurt pushed past his friend, dragging her behind.

Clint followed and closed the door after they'd crossed the threshold. The quiet of the interior was a bit intimidating. Tony walked down the stairs with another man, who she guessed was Colt. Colt was younger than Tony, but the way he clung to the older shifter spoke volumes about their relationship. Seeing that Colt was indeed back safe and sound made Savannah feel so much better. Even though Kurt had told her he was back, Savannah liked seeing it with her own eyes. She could tell Rudy that his information had indeed helped and that Colt was safe.

"You must be Savannah," Colt stated as he and Tony reached them. "Tony told me what you did for Rudy and I wanted to thank you."

"No thanks necessary," she assured him. "I'm just glad you were found."

Colt nodded. "Me, too. When Rudy warned me about Bruce, I didn't want to take the chance of contacting Tony. I was worried they'd somehow bugged my phone or something."

Tony growled as he tightened his hold on Colt's waist.

"Which was stupid," Colt said with the roll of his eyes. "I know. And I'll never do it again."

Colt's words sounded rehearsed, but Tony relaxed next to him. There had probably been a long discussion about what Colt had done and why Tony was not happy with him. Savannah knew that if she'd been in Tony's shoes, she'd have gone insane had Kurt gone missing.

"I had coffee, tea and some pastries taken to one of the large conference rooms. Our friends from Arizona should be there already and the sheriff is pulling up now," Tony said.

"I'll wait for the sheriff," Clint offered.

"Trying to earn brownie points?" Kurt teased.

Clint flipped him off and Savannah was utterly amused by the two men. They had such a great relationship. She was a little jealous that she'd lost the contact she'd once had with the people in town. Savannah was reconnecting with Sara and that was a start. Plus, Kurt made her feel welcome with his group.

Tony and Colt walked in front of her and Kurt as they traveled down a long hall. The portraits on the walls were all of distinguished-looking older gentlemen.

"The Council members," Kurt whispered in her ear. He slowed down until they came to a stop in front of the last one. "That's Alpha Babcock. He's the one who brought me and Clint in. He's a good man. If you ever need anything and can't get hold of me or Clint, you should go to him."

"Is that a possibility?" she questioned. "Not being able to get to you or Kurt?" Savannah didn't like the sound of that.

Kurt shrugged. "You never know. I just want you to be aware of the options just in case."

That left Savannah a little unsettled, but she nodded then allowed Kurt to lead her away. There was a low murmur of voices as they entered the conference room. There must have been something in the water that shifters drank, because the men in the room were more than just a little attractive. She peered over at Kurt, who was grinning at her.

She found herself blushing. There was no way that he knew what she was thinking. Besides, Kurt was still the hottest man in the room.

Kurt bumped her side before throwing his arm around her shoulder. "It's okay," he murmured. "I know you still like me best."

"I do," she told him.

"But they're attractive," Kurt whispered. "You're mine though."

"And you're mine," she quipped back.

"Hello." The big blond closest smiled at her.

"Hi." Savannah gave him a little finger wave.

"This is Savannah. She's a deputy and has been helping with the investigation into the church," Kurt said. "Savannah, this is Cody, Zak and Jamie. The shifters who rescued Colt."

"It's nice to meet you all," Savannah greeted.

"It is very nice to meet you," Jamie replied. He stepped closer and held out his hand.

Savannah shook it as Kurt tightened the arm around her neck.

Jamie grinned wider, which had Kurt growling. Savannah glanced between the two men. "What?"

"She is with me," Kurt declared.

Pride rushed through her at Kurt's words.

"Yeah, we caught that by the possessive hold you have on her," Zak responded. "It's okay, man, we don't poach."

Kurt couldn't be jealous. He was the one who'd wanted to introduce her to these guys and had joked when they'd first entered the room.

Kurt huffed. "I know. I just wanted it to be said."

"Well, I don't blame you," Cody said. "Beautiful and smart." He shook her hand. "I've heard how you and the sheriff gathered the intel that is going to put Dan Carter away."

"We're going to try," she replied.

Tony and Colt had already sat. "Why don't we take a seat? Clint should be bringing in the sheriff."

Kurt ushered her over to the long conference table and she found herself sitting between him and Tony, the out-of-town shifters across from them.

Clint rushed in with the sheriff at his heels followed by the older gentleman that she'd seen the portrait of. Alpha Babcock.

"Good, everyone is here." Babcock took a seat at the head of the table as Clint and the sheriff settled down on the other end. "I see there is some food and coffee. I believe we are going to need it."

Kurt passed her a steaming mug of coffee and she wrapped her hands around the hot cup. The fragrance of the strong brew wafted up from the mug and she took a small sip. *Oh, heavenly.*

"This is good coffee," Jamie declared. "And I should know. I drink enough of it."

"It's from the local coffee shop. We get special delivery." Babcock nodded toward Clint.

Of course it's Sara's brew. The Council would support the hometown shop and Clint's partner.

"I'll make sure you have some to take back to Arizona with you," Clint offered.

"Appreciate it," Jamie said before he took a long drink.

Guess the hot temperature doesn't bother him. Another thing that must be nice about being a shifter. Savannah could appreciate the unique abilities each shifter had, but the hate directed at them took away from the enjoyment of what she was learning. Humans hunting animals in protected lands and ending up killing shifters by accident had been a main cause of why the shifters had come out. Now shifters were being hunted down on purpose. Savannah might have been human, but she was ashamed of how some other humans were reacting.

To her, it was a gift to know about the shifters. She also wondered what else was out there. Kurt set a plate with a muffin and pastry down in front of her. Savannah had gotten lost in her thoughts and hadn't noticed everyone else getting their snacks.

"Where should we start?" Alpha Babcock asked.

Sheriff Webb nodded. "The FBI will be here later this morning. They will take over the case since it involves several divisions of the Church in different states."

"Will they actually believe us?" Clint asked. "The FBI hasn't had the best track record of protecting shifters."

"Rumors," Alpha Babcock corrected. "We don't know that the FBI is on the side of the Church and humans like them."

"We've had the same problem," Cody stated. "Anytime we work with the federal agencies, they don't take any threat against the shifters seriously."

Alpha Babcock nodded. "However, I called in a favor. The agent coming is a shifter himself. I think that will ensure that the investigation is followed through on."

Kurt blew out a breath. "Wonderful." He looked over at Savannah and smiled. "That's great news."

She agreed. If the agent was a shifter, he had to understand the threat that Carter posed.

"But that does bring up the subject that Kurt has brought to my attention. I've spoken with the Feline Prince and several of my other contacts within the shifter communities. It's been agreed upon to start talking about having an agency of our own. One made up of shifters."

"Is that even possible?" Sheriff Webb asked.

"Yes." Tony nodded. "The need for our own government agency was brought up when we first discussed going public. At the time, it was decided to hold off to give the human authorities the opportunity to prove they accept us."

Colt snorted. "That hasn't exactly worked out as planned."

"No shit," Clint agreed.

"It's not like we knew the humans would band together to take us out." Tony glared at Colt.

"It doesn't matter any longer," Alpha Babcock declared. "It will be rectified."

"I'm interested in what the plan is," Cody said.

"Good," Alpha Babcock stated. "I want to talk to each of you about a position with the new agency. We'll need strong shifters who have experience in law enforcement." Alpha Babcock glanced at Kurt. "Or military."

Kurt nodded and despair went through Savannah. A new agency for shifters would take a lot of time and would be a big responsibility. She also doubted that the agency would be based in her town. Which meant this opportunity would take Kurt away from her.

Not that Savannah could blame Kurt for wanting to take part in the agency he would have a hand in building. Kurt was smart, strong and intelligent. The shifter agency would need him and it wouldn't be fair for her to hold him back.

As the shifters continued to discuss plans and what needed to be done, Savannah sat back and listened.

She was losing everything that she thought she'd finally gotten. Kurt had claimed her in a relationship, but that was with him staying there with the Council. When he moved, Kurt would be too busy to worry about her, a human.

The first hour passed and Savannah began to feel more and more out of place. She didn't belong at the table. Not only could she not add to anything that the shifters needed, because she didn't know, but the more the plans came together, the closer Kurt would be to leaving her.

"How about we take a break?" Alpha Babcock suggested.

Savannah glanced up. *Yeah, I can use some air.*

"I'll call Prince Zachary and see where he is. He shouldn't be too far away," Tony said as he stood.

"I need to get back to the office and wait for the FBI," Sheriff Webb stated.

Savannah rose as well. She needed to go with the sheriff. At least working with the FBI gave her a way to help the others. Plus, she couldn't sit next to Kurt as he strategized and organized a life without her.

"Hey." Kurt caught her hand. "Where are you going?"

Savannah smiled down at him. The least she could do was make things easy for him. "I need to go with the sheriff. The FBI will want to talk to me, since I was the one who collected the evidence."

"Oh." Kurt frowned. "But you're okay?"

"Fine," she lied. Savannah leaned down and kissed him gently on the lips. She straightened then peered around the room. The Arizona shifters were huddled together talking, Clint was walking the sheriff out and Tony, Colt and Alpha Babcock were already gone. "I'll see you later."

"How about you come by my house tonight?" Kurt asked. "I'll pick up dinner."

Oh God, she was trying to put distance between them and Kurt was going to make things hard for her. She nodded but didn't manage to say anything. Savannah quickly walked out of the room and down the hall she'd come through.

She caught up with the sheriff at the front door.

"You're leaving?" Clint asked with surprise.

"There is a lot of work to do at the station," she told him. "I need to make sure all the reports are complete to hand over to the FBI."

Clint nodded. "Sure."

Sheriff Webb patted Clint's back. "Just make sure you email the statements from Nevada, including the ones from your new friends."

"I will," Clint promised.

Savannah had heard enough. She slipped past the sheriff and Clint and exited the building. The freshness of winter and bite of cold felt good. Standing on the steps of the compound while peering across the large property, Savannah didn't think she'd be back.

The way Alpha Babcock was talking, the shifters were going to be moving quickly on setting up the new agency. Kurt would need to move soon. There had to be a way for Savannah to avoid getting involved any further with Kurt. If asked, she'd have to admit that she had fallen in love with him. She loved him. And it was going to hurt to say goodbye.

"Ready?" Sheriff Webb stepped beside her and pulled at his collar.

"Yeah," Savannah said. She wanted to get out of there.

The entire drive through town, Savannah kept her thoughts to herself and didn't speak. The sheriff wasn't inclined to talk either, so she was able to plot how to evade Kurt for a few days.

"We're here," Sheriff Webb announced. He pulled into the parking spot in front of the back door. "Now do you want to tell me about what's bothering you or go inside and wallow a little longer?"

Savannah smiled. She just had to. Even though she was heartbroken that her future wouldn't be what she'd been dreaming about, she still had good people by her side. In her hometown. Where she would have a life, one way or another. "I'm good."

She didn't wait for him to say anything else. Savannah pushed the door open and stepped out into the cold. This time she didn't enjoy the rush of winter. She was chilled from the inside now. It would be lonely without Kurt, but Savannah would recover. He had important work ahead of him. In order to protect the shifters like Clint and Ryan and all the others, Kurt needed to follow through with his idea. The back door opened and Ryan smiled out at her.

"I saw the two of you pull up on the cameras," Deputy Jacob Monroe said. "Thought I'd open the door and get you into the warmth."

"We appreciate it," Sheriff Webb said as he walked past her.

Savannah followed the two men inside and walked right to her desk in the middle of the room. The only one who had their own office was the sheriff.

"Any word from the Feds?" Sheriff Webb asked Jacob.

"Not yet, sir," Jacob answered.

"They should be here soon though." Savannah pulled out her chair and sat. She reached for her laptop and turned it on. There were hours of paperwork ahead and she needed to do her part and help the man she loved take down a true monster.

* * * *

Kurt stared out of the window of his office, clutching his cell phone. Savannah hadn't returned any of his messages and he had a really bad feeling about why. She'd closed herself off to him during the meeting. Out of nowhere, she'd gone from excitement and wonder to blocking her emotions. He didn't even know if she was aware she'd done it.

"I take it you haven't reached your lady friend?"

He turned to where Alpha Babcock stood at the entrance of his office. "Hello, Alpha."

Alpha Babcock dipped his head.

"No, she hasn't answered the phone," he admitted.

"Well, she does have a very important job," Alpha Babcock stated. He walked over to the chair and sat. "An entire town she protects."

"I know," Kurt responded. But it had been a long-ass day of planning, negotiating and organizing the future for the shifters. He'd hoped to order dinner and pick it up before meeting Savannah at his house. That had been hours ago. Now Kurt was avoiding going home because he didn't want to be alone. He followed suit and sat next to Alpha Babcock.

The Council members weren't known for being the type to just come and hang out, so there had to be something the Alpha needed.

"Is there something I can help you with?" Kurt asked.

Alpha Babcock smiled. "I believe it's my turn to help you."

Frowning, Kurt leaned forward. "I'm sorry? Help with what?"

"Do you plan to take one of the positions with the new agency?" Alpha Babcock asked.

Kurt jerked back. "No." *Oh shit, is that what the Council wants?* Kurt had just started making a life for himself there. He had his friends, a great position with the Council and Savannah. If they were offering him a new job he'd have to turn it down. "I mean, I appreciate the offer—"

Alpha Babcock waved his hand. "We don't want you to accept another position. We're quite pleased with what both you and Clint have brought to the compound. We'll still need you. While I'm glad we're moving in the right direction for all shifters, our first priority is our wolf packs."

"Then why'd you ask?" Kurt questioned. He had a headache and this conversation was not helping.

"Because it wasn't said in the meeting this morning," Alpha Babcock said as he leaned forward. "So, some of the others around the table might think you're looking forward to a new adventure."

That was when it dawned on Kurt what Alpha Babcock was telling him. "Damn." He thought Savannah knew he was sticking around. He'd been making plans for a future for the two of them. Hadn't he been clear that she was the one for him?

Alpha Babcock reached over and patted his arm. "When it comes to matters of the heart, I've found, one's imagination can go wild. You just need to talk to your lady and make sure she knows where you stand."

Kurt nodded as he rose. "Yes, I'll do that."

"Good." Alpha Babcock stood then headed away. He paused at the door and looked back at Kurt. "I've watched you since you first arrived. I like seeing you happy and settled. Don't be afraid to go after what you want."

"Yes, sir." Kurt watched until Alpha Babcock was out of view. He didn't know why he hadn't figured out what might be wrong with Savannah on his own. Maybe it was because he was already so sure of his relationship with her that he hadn't thought to be clearer about his intentions. But he could fix that now.

With determination, he stalked his way across his office and out through the door. He made it through the long corridors of the compound without seeing anyone until he reached the front door.

He froze, sure that his eyes were playing tricks on him.

Savannah stood by the front entrance shaking snow from her coat as one of the guards looked on. Kurt cleared his throat. The guard jumped while Savannah just peered up at him.

The guard blushed before dipping his head to Kurt. "I was just letting her in."

He was admiring her, but Kurt couldn't be too upset. She was beautiful, especially with the ice flakes still on her eyelashes and in her hair.

"Thank you," Kurt replied to the guard. "I'll take it from here." Fuck, he was so happy to see Savannah. It took all his control not to rush over and wrap his arms around her. He never wanted to let her out of his sight again. Not if she doubted how he felt.

"It's starting to ice over," Savannah told him. "The roads are going to be a mess in a few hours."

Kurt wasn't sure how to respond. What was she doing here? Why hadn't she answered his calls or texts?

Savannah straightened her shoulders before taking a step toward him. "Can we go into your office? To talk?"

"Talk," Kurt repeated. He didn't want to talk. Okay, he didn't know what he wanted, but it didn't matter. Kurt was just so happy to see her.

"Yes, please."

She was holding herself too stiffly. He didn't like seeing her like that. But it had to mean something that she'd come to him. Kurt would assure her that he wouldn't be leaving and that everything was going to work out. Before she left his office, Savannah was going to know how he really felt.

"I'll make some coffee and we'll get you warmed up as we talk," he said. Kurt held out his hand and offered it to her.

Savannah stared at his palm for several moments before she reached out and intertwined her fingers with his. That was a start—at least he was touching her. Kurt gently tugged her toward down the hall.

The quietness of the compound was almost eerie, but he was happy that they would have some privacy. Clint had already left for the night and the Alphas would be in their own residences. That left just the few guards currently on duty. He still closed his door after they'd entered.

"Why don't you sit and I'll get the coffee?" he said.

"Sure."

He ignored the nervousness coming off her as she rubbed her hands down her pants while crossing the room. Savannah didn't need to be nervous. Not around him, ever. Using the Keurig, he quickly made her a cup of medium-blend coffee. It wouldn't be as good as what she'd have gotten from Sara's shop, but it should begin to warm her. He hoped to be able to provide any more needed heat.

She was sitting with her knees pressed together and head down as he reached her to hand her the mug.

Their fingers brushed and he smiled at her.

Savannah took a deep breath before she grinned.

Chapter Ten

Savannah wished her fingers weren't shaking when she took the hot cup of coffee from Kurt. She hadn't planned to come to the compound, but she just couldn't stop herself. Kurt had called twice after sending a series of text messages about dinner and she'd been strong and ignored them. But, driving home, she'd found herself passing his house, which had been dark. She'd known he was still at the compound, so instead of turning around, she had driven to the compound.

At the gate, she'd wondered if she'd even be let in.

She hadn't had any trouble. As soon as she'd rolled down her window, the guard had smiled and waved her forward. Savannah had been nervous, but she'd made it past the gate so she'd kept going. It was obvious that she'd surprised Kurt.

Now, with him sitting next to her, Savannah was losing her nerve. At first, she'd figured that she could avoid him until he left, but just the thought of not seeing Kurt again hurt. She needed to confess her love and let him decide if that was enough to keep him there, with her. Savannah didn't want to hold him back, but if also wasn't fair to allow him to leave without having all the information.

"So." She blew into the mug so she'd able to take a drink. "I have something I need to tell you."

He opened his mouth. Savannah shook her head though. She needed to get through her rehearsed speech.

"Please let me say this."

Kurt frowned before sitting back in the chair, then nodded.

She sipped her coffee, giving her the few seconds she needed to gather her nerve. Savannah pulled the mug away from her lips then looked Kurt in the eye. "I love you."

He gasped.

Savannah wanted to smile but needed to finish what needed to be said. "I knew right away that you were going to be something special to me. I thought it would take more time, but just the thought of you leaving makes me want to tear my heart out."

"Savannah—"

She shook her head. "I feel horrible that I'm doing this to you, but I couldn't let you go without telling you one time that I fell in love with you. I don't regret it and I never will."

He moved so quickly that she jerked back, spilling the mug onto the carpet. Kurt caught the falling cup and tossed it aside, making a bigger mess. When he gripped her chin, forcing her gaze on his, she didn't tense. "Don't you know that I would never leave you?" he asked in a whisper.

"But—"

"No, baby," he said. "I'm sorry that you doubted for even a moment that I would leave you behind."

"I can't go with you," she said. It hurt to speak the words, but she needed him to understand. "I've thought about it, a million times probably, but I am needed here."

"As am I," he told her.

Savannah bit him lip as she tried not to let hope grow.

"I was never leaving. I thought you knew that. I'm sorry that you didn't," he said. "Yes, I'll be very involved in the start-up of the new agency, but my work will be done from here."

"You're not leaving?" she asked. Savannah needed to hear the words again.

He lowered his hands, running them down her neck, then over her shoulders, and finally gripped her palms with his. "I'm not leaving."

"You're not leaving," she repeated. Had these hours of hell been for no reason? No, no way had she misunderstood what had happened that morning.

"I have a job here that I like. My position with the Council is one of the highest in the country. I wouldn't give that up to work for a federal agency for little money and no respect."

Savannah did grin at that.

"I love my house here," he continued. "I want to add on to the existing structure. Plus fix up the back a little more. How does a hot tub on the deck sound?"

"A hot tub?" Savannah could already picture the two of them cuddled in the steaming water, naked, relaxing together.

"I think our house definitely needs a hot tub," Kurt told her.

"Our...house?"

Kurt raised her hand and kissed each finger. "Our house. I want us to be together all the time. You told me that you love me. I've known that I loved you for a while now. We'll protect this town together."

He was saying all the right words.

"Stand up," she demanded.

Kurt frowned at her.

Savannah pushed him back so she could rise and stand toe to toe with him. "We'll protect this town together and live in your house, under one condition."

"And what's that?" he whispered with his lips just inches from hers.

"You take the rest of the weekend off. We go back home, to our home, lock the door and don't answer the phones."

Kurt barked out a laugh. "Is that all?"

She shook her head. "It won't be easy. I'm supposed to be dealing with the FBI, you have out of town shifters, and we are still waiting for Carter to be arrested. But can you give me two days?"

"I can, but I have one stipulation to add," he told her.

She narrowed her eyes. Kurt was running his fingers down her side. His touch was both distracting and electrifying.

"We don't have to wait until we get home." He tightened his fingers before he yanked her against his body.

Savannah merely smiled before she grasped the back of his neck, forcing his mouth to hers. She nibbled on his lower lip until he moaned and opened for her. Kurt was right. They didn't need to wait until they got home. They could reconnect right there first before she had him for a full two days. She knew she was asking a lot. There was so much to plan for and they both had important jobs. But she needed to prove to herself, and Kurt, that they would always be able to put each other first.

His kiss had all the nerves in her body singing.

She felt alive.

And she belonged to him. Just as much as he belonged to her.

Savannah ran her palms up his back and gripped the soft material of his shirt, pulling at the garment. She wanted him naked. Craved to feel and taste his flesh. She pulled back so she could attack the buttons.

Kurt wasn't waiting patiently, either. He was tugging at the snap of her jeans.

It was a mad dash for both of them to get the other naked. Savannah laughed when their arms got tangled up.

"I've got to feel you," he whispered.

"Me, too." She pushed Kurt onto the couch before following him down. Savannah straddled his waist, his cock hard and leaking against her leg, as they kissed again.

His legs were hanging off the edge of the cushions so she had him trapped under her. Savannah ran a finger down his chest but stopped when she reached his smooth, hard stomach. *Damn, Kurt has a* nice body. And she was going to be able have his awesome body any time she wanted.

Savannah leaned forward to run her tongue on the same path her finger had taken. She lapped up the saltiness of the sweat on his skin. Kurt moaned while bringing his hands up to her hips and gripping her tight.

She peered up at him. "I love having you at my mercy."

"And I love being here, like this."

"Good." For his response, she let her body slide down his, rubbing against his hard cock, before she was between his legs. Savannah gripped his shaft and pumped him a few times then leaned forward and licked up the pre-cum from the tip of his cock.

Kurt closed his eyes before letting his head fall back into the cushions. His legs were trembling where they had her pinned in.

Savannah kept her gaze on his face. She lowered her mouth, taking him inch by inch.

"Yes," Kurt hissed.

Not wasting any more time, Savannah licked, sucked, and jacked Kurt until he was pushing his cock down her throat. He was still being just a little bit too careful. She wanted her man to lose control.

With a wicked suck, Savannah finally got what she wanted.

Kurt plunged his fingers into her hair, held her head and began to thrust quickly. Savannah relaxed her throat. He plunged a dozen times more before he pulled back and tugged her into his lap.

He panted while positioning her until she was hovering over his shaft. "Ride me," he demanded.

Like she was going to argue with that order.

With her hands braced on the back of the couch, Savannah lowered herself down. Kurt's cock filled her slowly and Savannah didn't think she'd ever felt more connected to another person.

"Look at me." He gripped her chin, forcing her to comply before she got the chance. "I want to watch you pleasure yourself on my cock."

She shuddered. That sounded so dirty and wonderful. Savannah nodded.

His eyes were practically glowing. It appeared that his wolf was close to the surface. Savannah didn't know how the connection between his wolf and human halves worked, but she wasn't afraid. She could never be afraid of him.

With his intense gaze watching, she picked up the pace and rode him faster. Harder. She bounced on his shaft, taking every bit of pleasure she could get.

"That's it," he encouraged. "Take what you want."

Oh, she planned to. Savannah rocked back and forth, up and down, until her clit tingled and her orgasm was close. "I'm—"

"Close," he finished. "Me, too. Make me come, baby."

Savannah rode him with all the energy she had left. She cried out as her climax was ripped from her. Kurt growled while thrusting up. He held her tight as he continued to plunge in and out. She let herself relax in his embrace as he finally came.

That had been fucking hot. Savannah could get used to visiting the compound, if this was what she had to look forward to. This was the second time they'd used his office for sex. Yeah, there were a lot of other places she could get her man to claim her on.

Kurt collapsed back and she laughed. He looked completely wrung out.

"You're going to have to carry me to the car," she told him.

Chuckling, he trailed his fingers down her sweaty back. "You should carry me. This is all your fault."

Who cares whose fault it is? Savannah was pleased with how the night had worked out. She didn't have to worry about Kurt leaving her. They were in this together. "I thought you wanted to go home," she teased him.

"Our home," he said.

"Yes," she agreed. "Our home."

"That you'll be moving in to as soon as possible," he stated.

She remembered the weather turning even colder and shivered. "How about I pack a couple of bags and stay over first?"

Kurt growled.

"Just until the weather warms up," she told him. "I'm not moving in the middle of winter. We can wait until it warms up some."

He was frowning. "As long as you spend every night in my bed. No more going home to sleep for any reason."

"Deal." She leaned forward and rested her cheek against his chest. "But we have to get up first."

"Yeah." He moaned but helped her sit up and his soft cock slipped out of her.

She blinked around the room before smiling. "I like it in here."

"It smells like us now," he said.

Well, damn, she hadn't considered the fact that the shifters would know exactly what had taken place in Kurt's office.

The look of satisfaction on his face, though, told her that Kurt was proud. Well, if he didn't mind, she wouldn't either. She rose and helped him to his feet.

Kurt bent and kissed her neck. "You smell like me too. I think you should always smell like this."

Who was she to argue? That sounded good to her.

Epilogue

Kurt glanced around the room and caught Savannah's gaze. She looked up from the punch she was pouring and grinned at him. It was a good night. All their friends were there celebrating Christmas Eve in the house that was now his and Savannah's home.

Since she had been renting, it had been easy for her to move in with Kurt. She'd wanted to wait until the weather cleared, but Kurt had been determined to get her moved in completely before Christmas. With the help of their friends, he'd been able to. That was all he'd asked for when questioned what gifts he wanted to receive for Christmas. Savannah was all he ever needed. Clint had organized their fellow shifters to get Savannah packed and moved in only a matter of days.

Her head had almost been spinning, but Kurt wasn't going to apologize. Once she'd confessed her love to him in his office that night, Kurt wasn't going to let her go. Ever. It might be too soon to discuss mating, but, as he peered around his house, he knew it wouldn't be long before he'd be unable to hold back.

This was just the first of many Christmases they'd be spending together.

The house was decorated beautifully. Red, blue and silver garlands and adornments were placed artfully around. Savannah had even hung mistletoe in the doorway of the living room. The light on the six-foot tree in the corner twinkled bright with the seasonal music playing low. It was a great party. He slipped away from where he'd been talking with Tony and Colt to make his way across the room to Savannah. She passed out two glasses then, seeing him, slid his way.

She looked gorgeous in a long black dress with silver lining. Silver hung from her ears and swung as she walked. Her long blonde hair fell in small curls down her back and over her shoulder. God, he wanted to slip away from the others and start the personal celebration.

Kurt growled low as she sidled up to his side. He wrapped his arms around her waist and pulled her close. "You smell good," he whispered in her ear before nibbling down her neck.

She laughed happily. "I smell like you," she teased.

It was true, but since she liked him marking her with his scent just as much as he did, Kurt knew she wasn't complaining.

"Can't help it," he told her. "Have to make sure all the men know who you belong to."

Savannah tilted her head back. "Trust me, everyone knows."

He chuckled. So they did. He didn't make any secret of his relationship with Savannah. He'd been working hard to get the new Shifter Coalition started. That was the name that had been decided for the agency that would be made up of shifters and police shifters. There were so many objectives for the Coalition agents that Kurt had high hopes for the service they'd provide. Savannah had been right there helping him every step of the way. She brought a steady and unbiased look to the agency.

His plan to have an alliance for all the shifters to help one another was coming together and had even grown more than he'd imagined. It seemed like every shifter they'd contacted had thought it was a brilliant idea. His outline had been picked up and expanded on. Governmental backing and Federal assistance would fund the United States Shifter Coalition.

There was still a lot of work to do, but he was happy with the progress they'd made in just over three and a half weeks. Positions had already been filled and local divisions were being built. Their shifter friends from Colt's rescue—Zak, Cody and Jamie—had all been offered jobs. The three shifters would actually be the first in the field for them.

It was a start in the right direction and Kurt was proud to be involved.

"What are you smiling about?" Savannah asked.

Realizing his attention had gone to his work, he shook his thoughts away. "You," he said smoothly. "I always smile when I think about you."

She slapped his chest, obviously not buying it. "No thinking about work." Savannah kissed his cheek. "This is our first Christmas together," she said, cuddling into his arms. "Why don't you think about that?"

He cupped her face. "I have been. We'll have many more Christmases together."

She hummed in pleasure. Savannah peered into the empty hallway behind him.

Kurt knew what she was thinking about, but they really couldn't sneak away. Something major was in the works. "Look." He nodded toward Clint. "He's going to do it." Kurt watched as Clint rubbed his hands nervously on his slacks.

Clint was looking over at Sara, who was laughing with Alpha Babcock and his wife, Jennie. Kurt didn't have to guess how Clint was feeling. He'd had a long talk with his best friend half an hour ago as he'd tried to calm Clint down. Kurt had no doubt that Sara was going to be beyond pleased with his proposal, but Clint was still nervous. Kurt couldn't see any reason why Sara would turn down the man she loved.

"Are you sure she doesn't know?" Kurt questioned Savannah. He'd gone with Clint to pick out the ring and had sworn Savannah to secrecy.

"No, she really doesn't," Savannah said excitedly. "This is going to be great."

Kurt agreed. He turned them toward where the activity would be and Savannah laid her head against his chest. He brought his hand up to caress the soft curls of her hair. Just being able to hold her gave him so much peace.

Sheriff Webb stepped into the middle of the room and held a hand up for silence. The room hushed around him and Kurt reached over to turn the music off.

"I want to thank everyone for coming tonight," Sheriff Webb stated. "I know this is not my house, but I asked Kurt if I could have a few minutes." He tipped his beer in Kurt's direction and Kurt nodded in appreciation.

"The last few months have changed this town and all the residents. Everything that we've been through was worth it, though. I look around the room at the new friends I've made and know I'm blessed."

He paused before holding a hand out to his daughter. Sara smiled questioningly but walked to him when he motioned her forward. He took her hand in his.

"I've also seen some beautiful relationships grow. I'm proud my daughter has found the man she was always meant to be with."

Clint stepped up and the sheriff transferred her hand into Clint's.

"What...?" Sara started to ask but gasped when Clint went down on one knee. "Oh, my God!"

"Sara Webb," Clint started but had to clear his throat. "I love you, Sara. From the first time I saw you standing behind that coffee bar, I knew you were the only woman for me."

Sara's eyes filled and Kurt gripped Savannah tighter against him.

"I'm asking you here tonight, in front of our friends and family, if you will marry me, and mate with me in the way of my people." Clint held out the ring he'd purchased the week before with Kurt by his side.

"Clint!" Sara sobbed his name.

"Will you be mine?"

"Yes!" Sara cried. "Yes, yes, yes!"

Everyone clapped as Clint rose and kissed Sara passionately.

"That was beautiful," Savannah sniffed.

Kurt agreed, knowing that when he asked Savannah he'd have to outdo his best friend. Because he would ask Savannah the same question one day.

One day not too far in the future.

He turned Savannah in his arms and kissed her tears away.

"I love you," he said quietly.

"I love you, too," she responded and kissed him.

"Now, let's go congratulate our friends." Kurt led Savannah through the gathered crowd to Clint and Sara's sides.

"You knew!" Sara accused. "You had to."

Savannah laughed as she embraced Sara. "I couldn't ruin the surprise!"

"I told you everything would be okay," Kurt told Clint, hugging him.

Clint nodded. "Shit, man, that was worse than going up against a dozen hostiles while bullets fly by my head."

Kurt chuckled but pounded Clint on the back. It had taken a lot of sacrifice and time for the two of them to be where they were.

They'd finally found a town that accepted them, the love they needed, and the future was bright. There might still be opposition from humans, but Kurt had faith that there were more good humans than bad. Savannah was proof of that.

She was human, and kind, and wonderful. He loved her. They were stronger together.

More of their friends came to Sara and Clint so Kurt pulled Savannah away from the crowd. They passed the guests of the party until they stood in the dark hallway. Kurt ran his hands down Savannah's slender back while holding her against his body at the same time.

"Merry Christmas, love," he whispered against her lips.

"Merry Christmas. Thanks for making all my wishes come true."

Kurt caressed her softly. "Always," he promised right before he kissed her passionately.

Want to see more from this author? Here's a taster for you to enjoy!

Shifter Chronicles

Hidden Hyena

Crissy Smith

Excerpt

The flashing blue and red lights illuminated the inside of the dirty, rundown convenience store. With blood coating his hands, Trent screamed into the radio for backup. Adam had gone so pale — Trent knew that wasn't a good sign.

"Please," he begged. "Please hurry." Where the hell is everyone? The other police officers should be here by now. "Where are you? Officer down! Officer down!" Trent shouted into the radio.

"Trent!"

Trent shot up in bed and gripped the arm of the person who'd been shaking him. "Mac?" His boss and best friend sat on his bed next to him.

"You were dreaming," Mac said.

"Screaming, you mean." Trent rubbed his hands over his face. The same nightmare, or memory, haunted him. The night Adam had died had been the worst of Trent's life. It didn't help that he kept reliving it.

"You want to talk about it?" Mac asked. He kept his voice quiet but had let go of Trent's arms. Mac already knew what had happened all those years ago. He was the only one Trent had told once he'd arrived in Brookside. Mac also knew Trent didn't like to be touched and Trent breathed easier when Mac stood, then took several steps away.

"No." Trent didn't want to talk. Or think.

"Okay, man," Mac said. "I'm going back to bed."

Trent waited until Mac had his hand on the door. "Mac."

Mac glanced over his shoulder.

"Thanks."

"I'm here for you," Mac responded. "Anytime."

All Trent could do was nod. He wished he could give in and be the man Mac wanted him to be. Mac believed the best of everyone who lived in the old bar and had become part of the family. But Trent wasn't ever going to open up like the others. He'd been betrayed too many times in his life.

Knowing he wouldn't be going back to sleep, Trent threw the covers off before climbing out of bed. He was already wearing a pair of sleep pants, so he grabbed his T-shirt off the top of the dresser and pulled it on before leaving his bedroom. The entire back area of The Den, a small bar in Brookside, California, had been made into small residences. Most of the shifters who lived there had done so for many years. They were the few people Trent considered his family.

He glanced at his watch. After four in the morning. The bar had been closed for a couple of hours, so everyone else should be in their rooms. Probably sleeping with no problems. Some of them would even be cuddled up to their lovers. *I'm not jealous, I'm not*, he told himself. It wasn't like Trent would ever have anyone to warm his bed for more than a few hours at a time. Good thing he worked in a bar. Plenty of opportunity to meet a woman, have sex and send her on her way. Trent was always up-front about what he wanted, so the females he slept with didn't give him trouble. A few showed up at the bar again, wanting him to take them to bed for another round, but Trent never slept with the same woman twice. He couldn't allow emotions to get involved. Luckily, most of the bed partners he picked understood the score.

Trent left the lights off as he made his way to the kitchen. He knew this place and while his shifter senses might not allow him to see in the dark, there were a few windows letting in enough light for his heightened eyesight to see.

Once in the kitchen, he turned on the small light above the sink so he could find his secret stash. Annabelle Sanchez, one of his favorite people in the world, always did a little shopping for the rest of them. Kelly, their cook, refused to allow them to eat anything processed or premade. But sometimes that was what they craved.

Opening the bottom cabinet, he reached back until his fingers brushed the top of a jar.

"Yes!" he hissed. Kelly sometimes found their stash and tossed the items. Not this time. Trent pulled out the jar of peanut butter. Kelly made an awesome strawberry jam which already had Trent's mouth watering thinking about it.

He made a peanut butter and jelly sandwich before cleaning up his mess. He did not want Kelly to find out he'd made himself a late-night snack. He'd never hear the end of it. Trent grabbed a beer before strolling out of the kitchen.

The back door led him to the quiet spot where Trent spent a lot of time.

He sat down at the picnic table and let the night settle around him.

Trent loved it out here. No one bothered him and he could stay for hours and hours. He loved to watch the sway of the tree limbs. The animals making a home inside the National Forest bordering their town would sometimes venture as far out as the bar.

In the shifter world, Trent's animal the lowest of the low. A hyena shifter was a joke to the other more popular species. To humans, Trent was a monster, an abomination. He'd never fitted in with anyone, not until he'd found a home at The Den.

But the natural animals that ventured this far reacted to Trent as if he were a predator. True, in his shifted form he had some crazy instincts, but he always had complete control of his animal side.

He ate his food while downing the rest of his beer. The others wouldn't be awake for at least six more hours. Just him and little critters he could hear skittering around. He needed to avoid thinking about the dream.

Adam had been his best friend since the day they'd been partnered together. Even after Trent came out to the public as a shifter, Adam's loyalty had never wavered. Too bad he couldn't say the same about his other friends or his lover. No one else had stood with him. And what had Adam gained by giving Trent that devotion? His death.

* * * *

Brookside, California. Melissa Bishop pulled her 2010 Titan truck up in front of the sheriff's office. She peered through her windshield at the old brick building. The blinds were open, so she could see the activity going on inside. Or a lack of activity.

There was a deputy sitting at a desk, but she couldn't see anyone else. It was still early. Just shy of seven o'clock in the morning. She wasn't due to report for her first day until eight, but Melissa had been anxious to begin her new life.

It had taken years and a lot of sacrifices to finally reach this stage in her career.

Melissa glanced at her hands. She was shaking. *Fuck, I need to get control of myself.* This was what she'd wanted. What she needed. The Shifter Coalition now worked side-by-side with the Brookside Sheriff Department. Melissa's chance to make amends started here. *Working side-by-side with shifters.*

Time to get started.

She pushed open her door, then leaned over and picked up her messenger bag. She stood and adjusted her khaki uniform. It was restricting and different. After the years of wearing the dark blue colors of the Los Angeles Police Department, she wanted this fresh start to work.

"Deputy Bishop."

Melissa spun around at the sound of the sheriff's voice. They'd only spoken on the phone, but she'd recognize the sound anywhere. "Sheriff."

Sheriff Magnus stood in the street, along with another man. They both held Styrofoam cups from the only coffee shop in town—Melissa had researched all the businesses around her new home.

Sheriff Magnus was a big guy, exactly as she'd pictured. The Brookside website reported him to be a tiger shifter. He'd been in charge of the Brookside Sheriff Department for three decades already. There wasn't a lot of information to be found on Magnus other than the website. He didn't even have a Facebook or Twitter account. She'd wanted to know her boss before taking the job, but he apparently didn't like posting pictures of his food.

The stranger wasn't as big as Magnus, but would still stand out in a crowd. Melissa had no idea how to tell what shifter species anyone might be. She didn't know if there was a secret to figuring it out or not. Hopefully she'd learn.

"You're here early," Magnus said.

"Anxious to get started," she replied.

"Fine." Magnus motioned with his cup to the other man. "This is Agent Logan Coldwell with the Shifter Coalition. I explained over the phone that we split an office with the Coalition."

"Yes, sir." Melissa turned to Agent Coldwell. "It's nice to meet you." He appeared to be pretty strait-laced. He wore a perfectly pressed blue suit.

"You, as well," Coldwell said.

"Well, let's go in. There's plenty of work to do," Magnus said.

"You're just mad because you have to meet with the park rangers today." Coldwell bumped Magnus as he started walking toward the office.

"Fucking assholes," Magnus spat.

Coldwell laughed. "I'll be there to make sure you don't kill them."

Magnus stomped forward, so Melissa hurried to follow along. She knew she had a lot to learn about working with shifters. She got the feeling these two men could fill in the missing pieces she sought.

Inside, the structure housing the Brookside Sheriff Department and the Shifter Coalition was disappointing. Instead of the large chrome-metal multi-floor office she was used to, her current job had her in a tiny building with crumbling concrete walls.

"Uh…" Melissa managed.

Agent Coldwell started laughing. "I told you it's ugly in here."

Magnus grunted. The fresh-faced young agent she'd spotted through the window glanced up and smiled.

"No, sir. No," she said. "It's…"

"Ugly," Coldwell repeated.

"It's a building that keeps the rain off our heads and allows us to do our jobs," Magnus stated.

"Yes, sir," she replied right away.

"Jesus," Magnus said. "Stop siring me to death. Call me Magnus."

Melissa stared at her boss. She'd never been allowed to call her superiors anything except their rank or sir. "Yes, s… Magnus."

"Good." He pointed to two desks covered in paperwork, where the lone deputy sat. "Those are taken." He motioned by the wall. "Take one of those. Drop your stuff off then come into my office."

"Yes, sir."

Magnus frowned at her.

"I mean Magnus."

He turned and stomped off to one of the two offices with glass doors and windows. Agent Coldwell had gone into the other office. Melissa strolled over where two desks were butted up against the other. Only a computer, monitor and mouse sat on each. Melissa set her bag down on the desk facing the door but put the offices behind her back.

Then she headed to her boss's office. She knocked on the doorjamb.

"Come in." Magnus lifted his head. "Sit."

He only had one chair in front of his large wood desk and she took it, then shifted around, trying to get comfortable.

"It's the worst chair I could find. Keeps people from coming in here just to blab."

"No blabbing, sir. I got it," she replied.

Magnus smirked. He pointed. "See that board?"

A white erase board hung on one wall of the sheriff's office. It was filled with numbers, a list of names, dates and status. "Yes."

"It's the reports of illegal hunting in the area in the last three months."

Melissa gaped at the board. "Only three months?"

"Each month there are more and more instances. This isn't only about hunting. There is some sort of conspiracy happening."

"That's why you're meeting with the park rangers," she hazarded a guess.

"Yes, although I don't believe it will do any good," Magnus said. "They don't want to get involved. They just tell me this is an issue a few fines can be given for."

"So you hired two more deputies."

"And pressured the Coalition to put agents in town," Magnus stated.

Melissa glanced over at the other office. Agent Colwell was on the phone while working on a laptop. His office, unlike the sheriff's, was filled with filing cabinets, boxes and clutter.

"You made waves in the LAPD," Magnus said.

Melissa sat up straighter. "Some would say."

"Everyone I spoke to said," Magnus responded.

"I pissed some people off." She looked her new boss in the eye. "And I don't regret it."

"So, tell me why," he ordered.

"I'm sorry?"

"There was something, some situation, which led you to the path you're on. I want to know what it is. And don't bullshit me."

"And if it's personal?" Melissa got the impression Magnus wouldn't give a damn.

"I don't care," Magnus said. "When I put the word out I was looking for two deputies, I received over forty applications. More than two-thirds were shifters."

"But you hired a human," Melissa said. She'd had no idea the competition had been so fierce.

"The other deputy starting this week is a shifter," Magnus said. "You are the only human who will be in this building. Will that be a problem?"

"No, sir," she replied.

"I'm taking a chance, allowing a human to protect an entire town full of shifters," Magnus said. "I did it because you made waves. Now, tell me why you did it. Why you applied with me for a position in this town in the middle of nowhere."

Melissa pressed her hands together. She already had the job. Magnus just wanted to know her story. Everyone had one, after all. She hated being in this position. Not that she blamed her boss — she was surprised Magnus hadn't asked her before. Melissa had thought carefully about her words and what she'd say.

"Have you ever heard of Detective Adam Cross?" she asked.

"No." Magnus leaned forward.

"He was a detective with the LAPD who worked in the gang unit. I'd recently been transferred to the missing persons division, but I knew him socially. He was killed one night after he and his partner stumbled onto a burglary at a local all-night store."

"A shifter?" Magnus had tightened his hand into a fist.

"Not him," she said. "His partner was, though. Adam could have asked for a transfer. It was common back then when the shifters...you announced your presence. If a human wanted a different partner, the request would be granted."

"I've heard some stories about LAPD," Magnus said.

"The worst ones are probably true."

"But Adam stood by his partner," Magnus stated.

"He did. It made him unpopular."

"But I bet it was even harder for the shifter," Magnus said.

Melissa dropped her gaze to her hands. Her heart hurt. "Yeah," she said softly.

"So, this cop gets killed and..."

"They walked in on a burglary and the guy panics. He shoots Adam and the partner returned fire. Perp is dead, but Adam is bleeding out."

"Jesus," Magnus said.

"Adam's partner is screaming on the radio for help."

"I have a feeling I know how this ends." Magnus rubbed his hand over his face.

"Dispatch waited to pass on the information. Available units waited to respond. Adam bled to death in his partner's arms," Melissa finished.

"Fuck," Magnus spat.

"There was a massive cover-up. The partner ended up walking away from it all."

"I don't blame him," Magnus said.

"A couple of months after everything had been swept under the rug, I heard a captain in my division talking about the incident. They called it an 'incident'. They blamed Adam for not bailing on his partner when he had the chance," she told him. "This captain had a copy of the radio transmission. I found it in his desk."

"You went into your superior's desk?"

"They were laughing about the death of a fellow officer," she defended herself.

"I would have done the same thing," Magnus said.

"After I listened to it, I couldn't put up with it any longer. It changed me. The desperation in Tr...the partner's voice. I will never forget it," Melissa confessed.

"So, you started making waves," he said.

"Yes."

"So, that's why I hired you," Magnus told her. "And I expect you to do the same thing here."

She snapped her gaze to his.

"There is something going on in my town. Now, I'm not saying the park rangers are involved, but if they are, I'll take them down. You're going to help me."

"I will." Melissa nodded. "Yes."

"Good," Magnus said. "Let me introduce you to Deputy Wilson. He'll bring you up to speed."

"I'm excited to get started," she told him. It was the truth.

"One more thing." Magnus rose from the desk.

"Yes?"

"Were you sleeping with Adam or the partner?"

Damn, how does he know? Melissa turned to face her boss. "The partner."

"The shifter," Magnus clarified.

She nodded.

"And what happened with him?"

"Nothing I'm proud of," she said.

Magnus walked over then shocked her by patting her shoulder. "We all make mistakes. But at least I understand more now. I'm happy to have you as part of the team."

About the Author

Crissy Smith lives in Texas with her husband, daughter, and three Labrador retrievers. The three dogs love to curl up under her computer desk and nap while she writes. It doesn't leave a lot of room for her but what's a woman to do?

When not writing or reading, she enjoys hunting, camping and shooting. But she has a girly side too and is addicted to pedicures and coffee.

She has been writing since she was a teenager and still loves everything to do with the paranormal. Her stories and characters all have a place in her heart. She loves the Alpha male, the dominant werewolf, and the Master vampire, which find their way in most of her books.

Learn more about the characters she has created at her website where they have their very own page. It will be updated from time to time to let you know what's going on with them. Also you can find out who will be in the next book.

Crissy loves to hear from readers. You can find her contact information, website details and author profile page at http://www.totallybound.com.

TOTALLY
BOUND

Home of Erotic Romance